HAADSAA

HAADSAA

VISH DHAMIJA

BLOOMSBURY

NEW DELHI • LONDON • OXFORD • NEW YORK • SYDNEY

BLOOMSBURY INDIA
Bloomsbury Publishing India Pvt. Ltd
Second Floor, LSC Building No. 4, DDA Complex, Pocket C – 6 & 7,
Vasant Kunj, New Delhi, 110070

BLOOMSBURY, BLOOMSBURY INDIA and the Diana logo
are trademarks of Bloomsbury Publishing Plc

First published in India 2025

ISBN: PB: 978-93-61312-96-0; eBook: 978-93-61317-02-6
2 4 6 8 10 9 7 5 3 1

Typeset in Minion Pro by Manipal Technologies Limited
Printed and bound in India by Thomson Press India Ltd

To my mum, Kusum Puri, and dad, Pushya Vibhooti Dhamija

SUNDAY, 7TH JULY

One

Where am I? I hear sounds that I can barely discern. White noise envelops me. Incoherent, garbled voices and indistinct muttering further intensify my already unbearable headache. There are people around me, that much I can grasp, but why I am surrounded by them and who these people are, I'm too far gone to deliberate. I seem to be on a gurney, being transported at a speed that makes my mind go fuzzier, if that's even possible. I feel nauseated; I can feel my bile rising. I should ask someone to pause for a minute, help me sit up, pat my back, let me retch. I try to murmur but no one seems to be listening, let alone stop and heed my whispered request. Maybe the words don't leave my lips, and my mind is playing tricks on me. Then everything becomes still and someone switches off the lights. Darkness engulfs me.

I wake up with a start to find myself delirious. My eyes feel leaden, my mind is still in a fugue, my body hurts like it's been hit by a cargo train. I open my eyes and my vision is blurry too; it feels as though I'm somewhere amidst the clouds. It could be possible that I have died and gone to heaven. It isn't helping that the room I'm presently in is quite dimly lit, and the only source of illumination is somewhere behind me. My first waking thought isn't at all different from the one I had before I faded out: where am I?

There's a digital clock on the facing wall. It displays three-thirty-one in bright red, oversized LED numbers. It doesn't specify a.m. or p.m. so I have no clue if it's morning or evening. On my left, close to my head, there is an IV stand holding a plastic bottle containing a clear liquid. A long tube runs all the way down into the cannula attached to the back of my left hand. The clear fluid drips into me at a slow but constant speed. The room is small, the walls are painted in ivory emulsion, and not substandard whitewash. An air-conditioner hums softly, but I can't see it. On my right, there are a few screens displaying digits in red and green, and a monitor tracking what I believe is my heartbeat; waves roll in and out as my heart beats through one cycle after another. A cable winds out from the monitors and is clipped to my right index finger. And on the right side, towards the far end, is the only exit to the room and the door is shut.

My tired, groggy brain manages to put all of this together to resolve the sense of disorientation bothering me: I'm not in any hotel, I am in a hospital room of a decent private hospital. And that's all I accomplish before I'm floating like a kite, the wind carrying me away. My eyes are gritty, my eyelids feel hot and heavy as if someone had placed heated coals on them. I dread closing them. I don't want to slip back into sleep. What if I never wake up? Moreover, I need to know, I want answers. I attempt to get up but my body plays Judas; I simply don't have the strength. I try to turn my head to check if there's a bell I can ring to summon a nurse or a doctor, but my head hurts. I realise I'm wearing a headband or a bandana. Surely that can't be it. Pain shoots up when I attempt to move my head. Must be a tight bandage. I want to yell, but no sound comes out. I feel weak, and tears well up. Why isn't anyone here? An attendant? Shouldn't someone be observing me when I'm in such a delicate state? What if I die? How will they know? Is there a camera in the room keeping watch over me? If yes, then maybe I could make some movements, and whoever is monitoring the feed might notice that I'm awake and send help.

The more I try to move, the more pain and exhaustion I feel. It feels like a losing battle. I close my eyes, take a deep breath to regain some strength to rise from the bed.

Five.

Four.

Three.

Tw…

Shadows. White-out. Pinpricks. Total void.

***

When I open my eyes next, the clock on the wall across from me displays seven-thirteen. I seem to have been roused by the not-so-faint squeak of the door. I hear soft footsteps approach me. A doctor has walked in. He's young, maybe thirty, certainly not older. Junior, probably. He's tall and good-looking with dark, thick eyebrows under rimless glasses. He is wearing the characteristic long white coat and carries the ubiquitous stethoscope around his neck. My eyes inadvertently shut. I have so many questions, but I want to wait and observe what he does. There is silence for a few minutes. Perhaps he is checking all the machines by my side. What if he merely takes the readings and leaves? No, I cannot afford that. I open my eyes.

'Good evening, Mrs Khan.' He has been watching me. So it's not the morning after, it must be the evening of the morning after. Or has it been longer? How long had I been out?

'Goo…eev-ng…' It takes a tremendous effort, and the words come out garbled.

'How're you feeling now?' He has a nonchalant smile on his face. He could be enquiring about the weather, with that tone. Can't he see the state I'm in?

I don't attempt a verbal response. I give him a slight nod.

'You've been through a lot, Mrs Khan. But you're safe now, you're in Max Hospital in Saket.' He offers a sympathetic smile. If he thinks that's enough to appease me, he couldn't be more wrong. If he can't even assess my condition, the amount of pain I'm in, what can I expect from him? As if reading my mind, he continues. 'I see that you're on the mend, Mrs Khan, but it might take a while to completely recover from the injuries and the trauma. Let me check your pulse.' He holds my right wrist in his hand and looks at his watch. Thirty seconds? Sixty? He puts my hand back and places the stethoscope on my chest. 'Take a deep breath, count to five and then let it go,' he says. As I do that, five times, he moves the diaphragm up and down my chest. It is a sharp reminder that I'm stark naked beneath the hospital gown. 'I have to acknowledge that you've made a miraculous recovery in a very short time, Mrs Khan. Most people in your state might take days, if not weeks, to be as stable as you are.'

'Wha…state?'

'You don't remember anything, do you?'

I try to shake my head.

'Don't move your head too much, please. You've got stitches on your forehead.'

The rest of his words barely register because I've closed my eyes. The events of the previous evening inadvertently start to play in my memory like a movie reel: my head banging against the mirror in our entrance foyer; the sound of a loud crash, still deafening my ears; the sharp pain, the splatter of blood. I can see shards of glass scattered all around me as my knees give way, and I crumple to the floor like a dress slipped off its hanger.

Then I run.

I can vividly remember what I was wearing – a baby-pink short sheath dress with four-inch stilettos and light make-up. Someone was coming over and, as always, I wanted to look my best for them. There was a lot of blood. A pool of blood. As much as I had wished for an attendant in my room only a while ago, I suddenly wanted to be left alone. I want this doctor – what was his name? Did he tell me his name? – to leave right away. I want peace and quiet. I don't want to talk. Not just yet. I decide to keep my eyes closed. In any event, how am I supposed to respond to a commendation that can scarcely be attributed to my doing? If my body was healing faster than someone in the next room, it has to do with a function of my cells or genes or immune system. He reads my silence as I want him to, thank God.

'I will leave you alone for now, Mrs Khan. I think you need to rest before we can talk any more.'

Talk about what? I don't ask, I've stopped acknowledging his presence.

'There is a red button on the table to your right side. Press the buzzer if you need anything, and someone will attend…' I hear him begin to say. Then he seems to be making a notation in a file and places it on the same table he mentioned a second ago. I sense him bending over me. I can feel his breath. Even with my eyes closed I can tell that he is waving his hand in front of my eyes to check if they are really shut. I don't fall for it; I don't respond. I want him gone. Then, the sound of his feet softly retreating from the room is audible. The squeal of the door confirms his exit. I let out a long breath, which I wasn't conscious of holding.

I want to stay awake, but I know I can't fight sleep.

Two

The gentle patter of rain outside wakes me up this time around. That, and the thirst. I don't feel hungry, but that might be because they are feeding me intravenously. However, I do have a bitter, metallic taste in my mouth. Maybe sucking on a candy would help. Where did that doctor say the buzzer was?

The nurse promptly responds. White, pristine uniform indicates she's just come on duty. I glance at the clock: it's nine.

'How may I help you?' she asks in a sweet, sing-song voice. She looks young enough to be in school.

'Water...please.'

She understands on the first attempt. She comes close – her name tag tells me her name is Shweta – presses a button on my bed, and the recliner raises my back. She stops at about forty-five degrees, and picks up a glass of water next to me, which I hadn't noticed till then. In any case, there was little chance that I could pick up the glass, raise myself up and have a sip, all on my own. She holds the glass close to my mouth and I take a few tiny sips. My throat hurts as I swallow.

'Thanks,' I say. 'Can I get anything to eat?'

She looks up at the IV bottle, and my eyes follow hers. A sticker below declares, in marker: *NIL by Mouth.*

'I mean…something to…change the taste in my…' I point towards my mouth. My throat hurts like someone's choking me.

She comprehends, nods and slips out of the room.

As I close my eyes I experience a sudden flashback of hands around my throat. Strong hands. Choking me. Struggling for breath...I bet there are marks on my neck still.

Shweta returns with the same young doctor in tow. This time round I'm feeling slightly better and flash him a smile. He smiles back. He, too, seems more convivial than last time. Then again, I'm more lucid and able to notice these things now than the last time he visited me, a few hours ago.

'How're you feeling now, Mrs Khan?' He addresses me as Mrs Khan again. I never changed my name after the wedding. I am Anushka Anand, but men assume every married woman takes their husband's family name. I have no strength to correct him.

'I've seen better days, Doctor…' I smile, but that hurts too.

'We like to see you smile.'

Oh, really?

'Shweta tells me you want something to eat?'

'Something…to…' I contort my face to indicate I've got a disgusting taste in my mouth.

'I understand.' He turns to Shweta who goes out again.

'What happened to me, Doctor—'

'Dr Aryan Yadav. Mrs Khan, I wasn't on duty when the ambulance brought you into the emergency late last night…' He picks up the file by my bedside to check. 'Actually, in the early hours of this morning.'

'Who was with me?'

'No one from your family, I'm afraid. I was told that you had called the police emergency service saying your life was under threat, and the ambulance and police rushed to your house in Sainik Farms. You were badly injured…' He looks at me sympathetically. 'You've had injuries to your head, and they gave you five sutures, but don't worry – there won't be any marks,' he tries to make a joke.

'You also have marks on your neck that correspond to your being asphyxiated with hands,' he adds, glumly this time. He's about to say more when Shweta returns.

She has a lollipop in her hands, which she unwraps and gives me.

'Thank you.'

'Please don't bite into it, just keep it in your mouth, and let the juices flow, Mrs Khan.'

He needs to stop calling me Mrs Khan, as if I were his aunt's age! If we had met under different circumstances, I would have even bet he's older than me. I'm only twenty-eight for heaven's sake.

Dr Yadav turns around, gestures for Shweta to leave, and waits for her to shut the door behind her before he continues. 'Your blood carried a heavy dose of sleeping pills, which along with the alcohol levels could have been fatal if there had been a delay in getting you to the hospital.'

I close my eyes. I remember the gin. Gin and tonic. I can feel a similar sweetness dribbling down my throat from this lollipop, but there is no burn in the aftertaste, no high.

'Any permanent damage?' I ask apprehensively.

'Oh no, no, no, none whatsoever. Nothing that won't heal. You will be as good as new in a couple of months, Mrs Khan.'

'Anushka. Most people call me Anushka.' And those close to me use Anush. But he isn't a close friend. Not yet, at least.

'Right. Anushka. What a coincidence that our names start with the letter A. You can call me Aryan, too.'

I want to tell him that even if the world were divided into twenty-six exact pieces, there would still be approximately 270 million human names starting with the letter A. And if Scrabble has taught me anything, it's that more words and names start with the letter A than with most of the other letters. But he's merely trying to be nice. I smile at him.

'Anything else I can do for you, Anushka?'

Is he leaving? Already?

'What else can you tell me about last night?' It's not that I don't remember; I can recall specific bits of the evening. But my memory has missing elements. It may be because I was drunk, despite my desire not to drink as much or it is possible that the drugs in my system had me blacked out. I could have done without those. Be that as it may, I want to know in case I'm missing something.

'Unfortunately, I have limited information at this time, Anushka. Also, this being a police case, I couldn't possibly tell you even if I knew.'

'Police case?'

'You don't remember anything at all?'

I gingerly shake my head.

'I'm very sorry—'

'For what?' If he doesn't know what happened, what is he being sorry for?

'No one should have to go through this.'

Oh, OK. I get it now. Tears cascade down my cheeks.

He waits for me to calm down before he says, 'I think it's time to say good night. I'll be back on duty tomorrow afternoon.'

'Could you stay with me for some more time?' He appears friendly enough.

'Of course I can…it's not like anyone back home is waiting for me.' He beams. He has a very boyish smile. I notice dimples in his cheeks when he does that, his lips parting to bare his perfect set of teeth. His eyes corroborate his smile. His cheerfulness appears genuine.

'So you don't have any family waiting for you, then?' I ask in an attempt to distract myself from the looming thoughts.

'No. I'm unfortunately single.'

'Why, *unfortunately*?'

'Well…I don't know, Anushka. Perhaps what they say is true – it might be a case of the grass being a shade greener on the other side.'

'So no girlfriend either?'

'No.'

'Friends?'

'Of course, everyone has a few friends.'

'Where are you from?'

'Bihar. And you?'

'Jamnagar. Tell me more about yourself.'

'Why do you want to know?'

'I don't want to be alone. I'm scared.'

'Is it about your husband?' he blurts out.

So he knows. I nod.

'What about him?'

He looks around. We are in this private hospital room, which is not much bigger than the walk-in closet at my house in Sainik Farms. There isn't anyone around. However, as I suspected, there is a camera. He looks in the direction of the screens that are displaying a series of graphs, images and numbers of my vitals. He walks back and turns one of the switches off. Then he picks up the only chair in the room and brings it close to my bed. I appreciate his discretion. How much does he know about me? I need him to reveal what he is privy to; I need to know what he and others in the hospital know. As he sits next to me, I can smell his aftershave – something with spice and eucalyptus. I blink a few times when I see him up close. He is handsome in a boy-next-door kind of way.

'The police are looking for your husband.'

'Did they not find him at our house?'

'He is absconding. By the time the police arrived at your property, he was long gone it seems. His car is missing too, so they'll definitely find him. There is nothing for you to be afraid of. In any event, he'd be mad to come here.'

'Surely, he didn't need to run, it's his property.'

'I don't know anything more, honestly. Whatever occurred at your residence might have reached the media after the morning news, and there was nothing on the news until I came on duty.'

'Why did Akbar have to run?'

'I'm sorry, but like I said, I don't know anything. Did you two fight last night?'

'We did, yes.'

'Well, it must have been a big one. You want to talk about it?'

'Akbar has been insecure from the day we got married. If I wear a backless blouse to a party, he gets jealous and slaps me when we are alone. If I colour or wear my hair stylishly, he accuses me of being coquettish and of trying to attract men to my "swan-like" neck. If I wear a sari, I am exposing my midriff. If I wear a dress, it is either too short or too tight or shows too much cleavage. If I wear make-up, I am a slut; if I don't, I don't care enough to look appealing for him. If I shave my legs, I'm doing it for other men; if I don't, I don't care for his desires. If I speak to a man at a party, I am a whore; if I don't, I'm being a snob-bitch. Heads he wins, tails I lose, I don't know what to do. He's seriously fucked up. More than me, really.'

'He certainly has a problem, not you. What makes you think that you're fucked up?'

'Can I have some more water, please?' The lollipop candy is over. I've been chewing on the plastic stick for quite a while now. 'Oh you don't know my backstory. Why would you?'

'I'm sorry, but I don't.' He gets up and brings me water.

'And I'm sure you're wondering why I wear backless blouses when I know my husband is the jealous kind.'

He doesn't respond but it's evident from his countenance. Every woman has a right to decide what she wears, and when. It's her decision. Not her father's. Not her brother's. Not her husband's. It's nobody else's business but hers.

'Because he likes it when I wear revealing dresses, and snaps photographs,' I explain. I can see that the revelation caught him off guard, like it would anyone else. I can see an expression of shock.

'Was he…was he—'

'Always like this?' I complete the question he has on his mind. Aryan nods.

'As they say, a serpent can discard its skin, but a snake's inherent nature doesn't change. I suppose Akbar was what he was, but he never exposed this side of him to me before we got married.'

I'm not sure he follows my analogy or metaphor. I see the clock on the wall. It's almost ten-thirty. Poor Aryan has been courteous, sitting beside me, listening to me babble for a while now.

'Tell me more about yourself,' I say. I have no reason to get to know him any better. But I don't want to be left alone in this hospital bed for the night.

Aryan tells me all. He comes from Ranchi, which is in Jharkhand, not Bihar, but I don't point that out. Old-timers who were born and raised in Ranchi still consider Bihar their birthplace, not the new state. He studied medicine and appeared for the Indian Administrative Services exam too, but didn't qualify. He continued to study medicine in his post-graduate programme and moved to Delhi. He takes his time and tells me the boring minutiae too, but I don't interrupt him. He sums up his mundane life story around eleven.

'What about you, Anushka?'

'Where do I begin?'

'From the beginning is usually the best start.'

I think about it. Then I tell him everything without reservations. Why? Even I don't know. Maybe I'm scared. Perhaps it's the effect of the drugs in my system.

Three

I was born in Jamnagar, a small town in Gujarat, about 300 kilometres south-west of Ahmedabad. It isn't small any longer, but it was quite a small town back then. My father, Ashok Anand, was a junior clerk in a private mill. It isn't wrong to be poor, but he had no ambition whatsoever. And that exasperated my mother, Priti. She was extremely ambitious. She wanted all the good things in life. And she was gorgeous. Not your next-door sexy but homely wife figure, she was glamorous – a proper film star/ramp model kind of beauty. Five feet six inches, slender and in shape, with dark hair that framed her face and ended at her shoulder blades. She had a diamond-shaped face – a narrow forehead and a small chin. She had pronounced cheekbones that sat high and elegant. She had small dark eyes which, contrary to the popular beauty bible, enhanced her attractiveness. She was incredibly sexy, if I may say so, because those who've seen us both together always tell me that I am a facsimile of my mum – which I take as a compliment.

She was fond of tying her saris really low, exposing her toned stomach. It was evident it peeved my dad – even I could sense it – but he didn't dare say anything. Never in my presence, at least. And that's not all. She had scores of boyfriends too. Maybe my dad knew and overlooked it, maybe he didn't have the balls to stop her from cuckolding him. But I knew. 'Uncles' came home after Dad left for work and I went to school. And despite my dad's frugal salary my mum always had money to spend on clothes, make-up, fancy jewellery, expensive lingerie, beauty treatments, haircuts and hair colour. Sometimes, when I returned from school, she was still *busy* with an uncle in her bedroom. *Just chatting,* she would tell me later. *Don't tell Daddy,* she would make me promise and give me extra pocket money. I believed her stories until I was twelve or thirteen years old, but as I grew older things became quite apparent to me. Yes, at times, I peeked through splits in the bedroom door. And see them naked, having sex. The men were using her, and she was enjoying them and using them back. It wasn't love. It was a transaction.

Akbar Khan was twelve years my senior. He was thirty-two when he saw me for the first time. I was beautiful like my mother, but I didn't want to live life like her. I wanted a better life, and Akbar came from an extremely rich family. He had distant cousins in Jamnagar, and he was at a wedding that I too had been invited to. He fell in love with me and I fell in love with his background, if I'm being honest. He wasn't Shah Rukh Khan or George Clooney, but he could pull me out of a penurious existence. If not for him, my parents would have found me an alliance from another small town. My future husband would have worked in some factory, and my dreams, like my mother's, would have to be realised by fucking scores of men.

Considering his financial background, the fact that Akbar was from a different faith didn't bother my parents. I was young, and yet smart enough to understand that the only religion in this world was money. I bet my parents would have thrown a fit when I introduced him, if Akbar had been as poor as us. Or if his family didn't have erstwhile royal *nawabi* roots in some small principality near the famous Pataudis. Money doesn't simply talk; it can also sing and dance and change beliefs. To be fair, Akbar was a lapsed Muslim as I was a lapsed Hindu – two of a kind: agnostics? He didn't insist I convert to his faith ever. Perhaps it was because Akbar wasn't answerable to anyone – his parents were long dead – so we started a long-distance relationship when he went back to Delhi after the wedding. He came to Jamnagar once a month and then proposed marriage to me after a year. My mum was even happier than me. '*You will be a princess,*' she said, tears rolling down her cheeks, and, cricket fan that she was, she told me, '*When kismet adopts you, you don't have to swing the bat hard to hit the ball. The ball drops into the arc of your bat swing.*' I could appreciate where she was coming from. Her daughter had achieved what she couldn't. He was loaded; I was a true copy of my mother: gorgeous. Only younger. It was a perfect Bollywood script. Little did we know, at the time, that it even had a twist. The twist was to come later. Much later.

I was studying law; I wanted to be a lawyer, but I never sat for the bar exam. My parents, who had forever told me they wanted me to grow up to become an independent woman, seemed to abandon those dreams right away. Working-class people like us always believe that life is merely a three-event thing for all humans: birth, wedding and death. But it's so much more in between.

After a simple wedding, I moved to Sainik Farms in Delhi with Akbar. To my small-town, lower-class, unaware mind it was a surprise that Sainik Farms had no residents who were war-decorated *sainiks* or crop-growing farmers. Ironically, there were no farms either. Instead, it had clones of English manor houses, French chateaus and Swiss-style chalets, complete with swimming pools and landscaped gardens designed to isolate each property from the neighbours and keep the financially elite residents away from prying eyes. The raison d'être of the isolated palaces, on humungous plots surrounded by gardens with overgrown yet manicured foliage, was to give privacy to the residents. However what most people aren't aware of is that this affluent, aspirational residential address in South Delhi is as desirable as it is unauthorised and illegitimate.

Akbar's house, on the ten-acre plot, was a dream. My poor father could never afford a property that vast even if he saved his entire life's earnings. The house featured more than 5,000 square feet of built-up area with Italian-marble floors, a swimming pool, cut-glass and Murano chandeliers suspended from high ceilings, Persian rugs, objets d'art that I scarcely recognised the value of, and expensive artwork on walls by artists I had never heard of. There was a fourteen-seater dining table for the two of us. In Jamnagar, at my parents' house, we had what you might call a dinette, a two-seater.

There were two full-grown tiger taxidermies on mounts – almost lifelike. Certainly acquired illegally unless they were from the time when hunting tigers was permitted in India, but I wasn't going to complain. He could easily have claimed that they were passed down to him by his ancestors.

Akbar's true colours started showing three months into our marriage. What I should wear, what I shouldn't. When I revealed too much skin. What made me look like a prolific hooker. What made me like my mother. To my amazement, he knew about my mother's indiscretions. He had hired a guy in Jamnagar to do a background check. It was quite distressing when he said he knew all about us, and alarm bells should have rung then, in retrospect. The knowledge that my husband had hired a private investigator to check on me should have spooked me, but I didn't react. I was enamoured by my new life in this new world, and this little violation of privacy didn't bother me one bit.

***

We take a break. Aryan's been patiently listening to me for quite a long time. He leaves to relieve himself.

'Are you sure you want to hear the rest?' I ask when he comes back, conscious that it's almost midnight. 'You have work tomorrow.'

'I'm not due back until two in the afternoon, so I will have enough time to rest when I get back. Anyway, if I go home, I'll read or watch TV. I typically sleep at around four in the morning. Just give me a minute while I grab a coffee.'

And so I continue.

***

Akbar controlled everything before I even caught on to it. He insisted I join etiquette and grooming courses. You have to understand that I come from a working-class background. I didn't know how to lay a table or how to eat properly with forks and knives. Or how to dress, or how to sit in a short dress. He had fallen in love with me because I was untamed and then he started house-training me to suit his needs. I resisted initially but eventually gave in. If I wanted to live in his society I had to follow the conventions.

Cracks began to surface in our relationship by the end of the year. If he was patronising in the beginning, he became quite dominating with time, but I let it pass as long as I hadn't come into myself as a woman. Then it was cloying. You don't always want to wear what your husband wants. You aren't bound to his choices. I shouldn't have to wear the kind of underwear he wanted me to wear. He believed that if I wore thongs it meant I was sleeping with other men. It became claustrophobic and annoying after a while. What parts of my body I should shave, how often – it was suffocating. Every time I told him to back off, he'd say I was acting like my mother, insinuating my mother's indiscretions with other men. I hated it.

Abhorred it. And then I invariably made it a point to challenge him. I started doing things that I clearly knew he would object to. I bought and wore shorter and shorter dresses. I started getting Hollywood wax treatments even though I knew he liked Brazilian. I jumped on every opportunity to peeve him. Truth be told, he seemed to enjoy my rebellion for a while. He saw it as a challenge. And the sex became intense.

It turned extreme without warning. Tying me up, smacking me, using toys, and before I knew it, he had become a full-fledged Dom – like a Dominant in BDSM. He dictated what I wore and did. And everything came full circle to where I was originally. He was controlling me. Only now it was in the bedroom, not in public. Believe me, it was worse because I was practically his puppet. He'd smack me painfully, the marks would remain on my face for days, and he'd decline any invites to dinner or parties rather than risk the chance of anyone seeing my marked face.

I lived this double life for a long time. I wore what he told me to, and rebelled at times. We had rows but somehow kept it going until we couldn't. And then he accused me of having an affair with his friend. His school friend, Rajiv Pant. He warned me that he'd kill both of us if he ever saw us together. And he was filled with rage when Rajiv came to visit last evening. He flew off the handle, ran to his study and pulled out his gun – and I know what Akbar is capable of. I was scared out of my wits. I know I should have stayed in the living room to talk, to argue, to convince him that Rajiv and I weren't having an affair. I wanted to tell him that Rajiv shows me respect, something Akbar doesn't. But he grabbed my neck from behind and banged my head against a mirror. My self-preservation instinct kicked in, and I ran into the bedroom and locked myself inside. I heard a single gunshot, but I had no idea if it was a warning shot or if something more sinister was taking place at my house. That's when I called the police. Akbar and I had been drinking since early evening – he made me gin and tonics. By the time the ambulance and the police arrived, I had lost consciousness.

MONDAY, 8TH JULY

Four

I open my eyes to see it's morning. At some point in the night, they must have changed the bottle, since the level of liquid in it is higher than the last time I checked. The clock across from my bed seems to be the only companion I have. It tells me it's eight-eleven. Memories flood in of my extended outpouring to Aryan, his nods and understanding. He is a polite man; he had no reason to entertain me but he did, and I'm thankful for that. I haven't the faintest idea how or when I stopped talking. I must have dozed off during a lapse in the conversation, and Aryan most likely thanked the Lord, took the opportunity and slipped out before I started on another rant. Didn't he say his shift only started in the afternoon? I wonder if he'll put in an application – if he hasn't yet – to be assigned to another area of the hospital. But somehow I know he won't. He is a gentleman, a bit too gullible if you ask me. Then again, I can hardly be trusted when it comes to reading people. Haven't I made blunders in my life?

A nurse comes into the room. Not Shweta who attended to me yesterday. This one is slightly older and seems a lot more confident. Cynthia, her name tag reads.

'How are you feeling, Mrs Khan?'

It seems everyone in this hospital has been given a script; they all recite the same words when they see me.

'I'm better.' I smile. She smiles back.

'The doctor will be seeing you around ten this morning when he comes for his rounds.'

'When will I be released from the hospital?' I want to be out of here.

'I am quite certain they will want to keep you here under observation for a few more days, but it will be the doctor's decision.'

'What if I want to leave?'

'Leave? Like now?'

'Yes.'

'You...can't,' she reluctantly responds. I can see the panic in her face. She knows well that no doctor can keep a compos mentis adult in hospital against their wishes. I can sign a self-release form and leave the premises any time I want.

'Let me call the doctor.' She rushes out of my room like Usain Bolt.

I'm not leaving, but I definitely will not be waiting another two hours to see the doctor. Aryan told me last night that this was a private hospital, and someone – most likely I – was footing the bill. The earlier I get out, the better.

A doctor rushes into my room with the same urgency as Cynthia. 'How may I help you, Mrs Khan?'

'Is Dr Aryan not in yet?'

'Dr Aryan works for me, I'm Dr Raaj Mehra.' He definitely looks older, and is surely more experienced if he's Aryan's senior or supervisor. 'Nurse Cynthia informed me that you want to leave?'

Why? Will it be too much financial damage if I do? 'I'm wondering how long I will be here. And where is my husband? Are you not allowing visitors?'

His smile disappears for a nanosecond when he hears my request. To his credit, he recovers instantaneously. 'I'm not sure if your husband is around, Mrs Khan.'

'What do you mean you're not sure? He is either here or he is not.'

'He isn't here.'

'Thank you.' I smile.

'You seem to be healing well.' He must have deduced from my speech and sarcasm that I'm feeling better. He takes my hand and repeats Aryan's performance from last evening.

Everything seems fine since he doesn't make any adverse remarks. 'The police would want to see you if you're feeling OK, Mrs Khan.'

'Can I see the police later?'

'You decide when you want to see them. If you're not feeling one hundred per cent fine, it's best to speak to them later.'

'When is Dr Aryan back on duty?' I ask instead.

Dr Mehra looks at Cynthia who promptly answers, 'At 2 p.m.'

'OK,' I say and close my eyes. I want them gone. I know I need to speak to the police. It doesn't matter whether you're the victim or a witness to a crime, the police are bound to see you. It was unavoidable under the circumstances. I postponed their visit since I don't want to be alone when they come to speak with me. And Dr Aryan Yadav and I had connected last night, I think. I might as well ask him to stay with me in case I get too anxious.

I hear their retreating footsteps, the squeak of the door, and I know they're gone. Then it strikes me. I should have asked when they'll take me off this stupid drip and give me something good to eat. I'll ask Aryan.

Five

I finally have a visitor. Monica Singh arrives around ten to see me. Cynthia ushers her into my room. Monica is married to Piyush, who is one of Akbar's friends. We only met after my wedding but she's my friend too, and a good one. I can trust her. But she's currently wearing an expression of mournful shock, as if her grandmother was just run over by a truck. She smiles sympathetically, sits down with her bag, and waits for Cynthia to leave.

'What's wrong?' I ask the moment we are alone.

'What's wrong? Why didn't you tell me anything ever?' Monica is the same age as me. She has big, round eyes the colour of wet sand, and straw-coloured hair to match. Born in Kolkata, she and her husband, Piyush, had attended the same school and were childhood sweethearts. I never asked when, how and where they met Akbar but I inherited their friendship through marriage. When I got married and moved in with Akbar I also lost all my childhood friends. Both my parents passed away shortly afterwards, leaving us no reason to visit Jamnagar. All the friends I have now are courtesy of Akbar. They were all his friends originally. It would be hard to keep track of the origins of all of Akbar's friendships. I'd never bothered to ask anyway.

'What are you talking about?' I am all too aware that the news of last night's violence might have leaked out, but I don't know the extent of it yet.

She pulls out a newspaper. We had made it to the section above the fold on the front page.

> **One Dead. One Injured. One Missing.**
> In a tragic event at Sainik Farms, a case of domestic violence escalated when forty-year-old Akbar Khan caught his wife, Anushka Khan, née Anand, with her paramour, Rajiv Pant. An anonymous source told our reporter that the affair had been going on for some time, and Akbar, finding the two at his own house, lost his temper and a bloodbath followed. Rajiv Pant's body was recovered from the living room at Khan's residence, while his wife, Anushka, was found locked inside her own bedroom. Her face was badly injured, and she had above-normal levels of alcohol and drugs in her system.
>
> Akbar Khan and his car were missing when the police and ambulance arrived at the scene. The police have recovered an unlicensed Glock .22 from the scene. Anushka Anand is in a private hospital, the location of which has not been revealed. She was unavailable for comment.

There's an accompanying picture of Akbar and me in happier times, evidently taken from the mantelpiece in our living room. There is an inset shot of Rajiv. Mercifully, they haven't printed a photograph of his corpse or the gore. Either that or the police didn't permit the media into the house.

I break down. 'Poor Rajiv. I know Akbar has a temper but to shoot another human being, his own friend...on mere suspicion...'

'I know, I know. Calm down, babe...everyone we know is shocked by the news. Rajiv was so affable, he was friendly with everyone.

How did Akbar even come up with this crazy idea that you were having an affair with Rajiv?'

'I don't know...I really don't. Maybe because he was the only single guy in our circle of friends.' I can barely talk. 'I can't believe Rajiv is dead because of me.'

'Not because of you, it's Akbar's doing.'

'Yeah, but I should have told Rajiv not to come over to our place since I knew Akbar had been suspicious of our relationship.'

'So Rajiv didn't know that Akbar had such misgivings?'

'No, he...he...probably walked in blind. He thought he was visiting his friends, and Akbar was as drunk as me, so he lashed out.'

'Oh God. This is a bloody nightmare.'

'How did the press get hold of the story? And who is this anonymous source who thinks Rajiv and I were having an affair, anyway?' I say it straight-faced, wondering how long I would be able to keep up my lies about the relationship.

'Now, now. Don't get stressed.'

'Where is Akbar?'

'Exactly like this paper reports: he's missing.'

'What do you mean missing? He's not some child who's been abducted.'

'He has obviously bolted, Anush.'

'How can he do that? He should be man enough to face the consequences rather than run away.'

'Don't worry, the police will get him soon.'

I break down. 'Where does it leave me, Monica? Accused of having an illicit relationship with a friend of my husband – who has absconded after killing my alleged lover?! The world must be thinking I'm some kind of slut.'

'Shh...don't even think about all that for now, babe. You need to recover from the injuries first.' Monica comes close and gives me an awkward hug since I'm still bed-bound. 'You're much stronger than a few mistaken allegations.' Monica can always say the right thing at the right time.

'Where's Piyush?' I ask after a few minutes.

'He's flying back from Mumbai as we speak. He's as shocked as us. He should be here by lunchtime.'

I close my eyes for a second. I can see blood flowing on the floor in a stream, I imagine Rajiv struggling after the shot, and then his lifeless body lying on the floor. I shudder and open my eyes in recoil. This nightmare is going to haunt me for a long time.

'What happened?'

'I don't know. In my mind's eye, I can visualise everything like it's a scene from a bad thriller, Monica – I can't let it go.'

'I hear you.'

'You can't even imagine how awful I feel...'

'I can't but I can appreciate it.'

Can she?

I bet the doctors at the hospital are still giving me sedatives because I can sense sleep taking over me. Or is it because I was up until late last night, chatting with Aryan? I can't focus for long. But I need answers to so many questions. 'What drugs were in me?'

'Drugs?'

'The newspaper says I had been on alcohol and drugs...alcohol I know about. How did drugs get into my system?'

'Who was making the drinks?'

'Akbar, of course. Who else?'

'Then he must have mixed them into your drinks?'

'Why would he do that? He didn't know Rajiv was going to visit us that evening.'

'We don't know what we don't know, babe. Maybe he knew, maybe he's the one who invited him over?'

'Why? Why would he do that if he actually suspected his wife of having an affair with the man? What kind of madness would make a husband invite her lover to come over?'

'Like I said, we have a lot of unanswered questions. We'll only know once Akbar returns.'

'When will he return?'

'Depends. If he's in hiding then the police have a job to do – find him, question him, bring him back. Where could he possibly be?'

'I know he inherited an ancestral property in Haryana, not more than fifty kilometres from here. It is his fort – the villagers worship their erstwhile nawab there. If he is there it will be impossible to get him since the villagers will be up in arms to save their prince. We have another property in the hills. In Kasauli, Himachal Pradesh. But that's a long distance from here, some three hundred kilometres, and considering that he was as drunk as I was, I doubt he could drive so far unless he had help getting away.'

'I'm guessing the police will know about these residences, and they are on high alert.'

'Driving to Kasauli on his own would be madness…oh, Akbar, what have you done?'

'If he drove up to Himachal, then he and his car are bound to have been captured on a camera at one of the tolls.'

'Monica, these folks at the hospital aren't being forthright with me. Can you sweet-talk someone to find out when I can go home, please?'

'I'll certainly check. You can come and live with us for a while.'

'I want to go back to my house…in case…in case Akbar returns and needs me.'

'Babe, your house has been cordoned off by the police. There are men and dogs searching every corner of the property.'

'Why?'

Monica raises her eyebrows and looks at me as if I'm stupid. I certainly am. Of course, it will be swarming with police. It's a crime scene. 'Do you have your mobile on you?'

'Yes, why?'

'Let's call Akbar. Wherever he is he'll take the call.'

Monica smiles at me like I'm mad.

'You think Piyush or I or the police haven't already tried that?' She pulls out her iPhone from her bag, taps the screen and turns it towards me. She had called Akbar twenty-one times. 'It went straight to his voicemail the first few times, and I left four messages. Later, I guess, with the police and everyone else trying to get in touch with him, the voicemail inbox got full. Now, it disconnects right away.'

'Maybe he is in an area where there's no signal?'

'Babe, this is the twenty-first century. You cannot be away from a mobile signal for so long—'

'Maybe his phone battery has died?'

'Same answer, babe. It's impossible not to find a place to charge your phone's battery. Moreover, if I'm not mistaken, Akbar is missing with his Mercedes, which has a USB port to charge his phone, so why hasn't he plugged it in yet?'

'Are you saying...?'

'Yes, babe. What I'm trying to say – and I know you will find it hard to believe – is that Akbar is hiding somewhere. He's likely deliberately switched off his mobile so that the police cannot track his location.'

'Can they do that?'

She rolls her eyes. 'Of course they can.'

I don't know what else to say, so I go quiet for a few seconds. Then: 'I think I have the landline numbers for his ancestral property and our house in Kasauli – they're in my mobile…'

'The police have already confiscated your phone and they must have found those numbers by now and called them.'

I have nothing more to say.

'Trust me, babe, the police aren't doing a perfunctory search. This isn't a missing persons case. Akbar's been gone for less than forty-eight hours and no one has reported him missing. Honestly, Akbar as a missing person might not even be a case as yet. This is a murder investigation. They will find him.'

I purse my lips to prevent myself from breaking down in sobs.

The door groans again. Nurse Cynthia is back to check on me. It's approaching noon. She checks my pulse, looks at the gauges, then smiles and leaves us.

Six

Piyush comes in ten minutes later. He looks tired. It is evident he's travelled here straight from the airport. He's the only one of Akbar's friends taller than him. He's six feet two; Akbar is six feet.

There is an inside joke between the two of them regarding their relative heights, a secret one. They call out, 'Two inches', every time they meet and laugh like six-year-olds.

'I'm so sorry to hear this, Anush,' he tells me. 'I had no fucking idea Akbar could do this to you.' He is referring to the injuries on my face. A battered wife. Everyone knows it isn't something that happens all of a sudden. There has to be a history for it to escalate to this level.

I break down in tears. Monica comes around and holds my hand to comfort me.

'I can't tell you how embarrassed I am, as a friend to you both, that I didn't have a bloody clue about all of this. If only I had any idea that Akbar thought you were seeing Rajiv I'd have drilled some sense into his daft brain. How can he even think you were playing around?'

Hearing my narrative back only makes my sobs grow louder.

'Stop it, Piyush,' Monica scolds her husband. 'We can talk about all that once they find Akbar. Maybe there's some misunderstanding—'

'Rajiv was shot point-blank in their house, his body is in the morgue, the gun used to fire the shot is in police custody, Anush is battered, and Akbar has skedaddled, and you still think there is a possibility of a misunderstanding?'

'All I'm saying is we don't know everything, so it's best not to jump to conclusions yet.'

Piyush looks stunned, and rightly so. His analysis of the situation rings true. I can bet the police are working with the same theory too: if he is in the right, why would Akbar go missing?

'Can't they find his car?' I ask.

'They've put out alerts to track it. It's a conspicuous car even if my asshole of a friend changes the fucking registration plates.' Piyush's language has always been peppered with expletives and mentions of anatomical parts. We're all used to it by now.

'Changing the plates would look like he was planning to run. He won't do that,' Monica counters.

'Well, just like you said a moment back…we don't know everything so it's best to wait for the police to do their jobs. Have they seen you yet?' he asks me.

'No, they're coming in after two today.'

'Do you want one of us to be around?' Piyush asks.

'I don't think it's required. The doctor treating me will be joining us.'

'Good. Stop the interview if you feel anxious or stressed. You know we are only a phone call away. If at any point you want a good lawyer, don't hesitate to ask for one. It's your legal right.'

'Why should Anush need a lawyer?'

'I'm just saying in case…' Piyush trails off. 'And we'll be back in the evening to see you.'

They bid their goodbyes and leave.

I ring the bell to call Cynthia and tell her I don't want to be disturbed for a couple of hours. I want to sleep. While it's good to see friends, it's also exhausting for me to keep conversation going in the state I'm in. Plus, the police are going to come in a couple of hours and I have to be alert when they question me. I'd better rest now. Cynthia totally agrees with me.

***

I have a feeling someone is with me and I wake up with a start. Dr Aryan Yadav is in my room. Handsome and smiling. In another life, under different circumstances, I wouldn't have minded going out for a drink with him. Maybe more, but that's irrelevant at the moment. *What-ifs* never did anyone any good. There is no other life, the circumstances are exactly what they were destined to be. People born in drudgery like me are not just short of cash, but of kismet too.

'Sorry, I didn't mean to wake you up.' He didn't need to apologise, his tone was considerate enough.

'It's OK, Doc. I wasn't going to sleep all day and then all night too.'

'Fair point. I can see you're starting to think more clearly.'

'You mean I talked total gibberish last night?' I flash a smile.

'You did sound a little strange at times, no offence.'

'None taken.'

'Good.'

'So how are my vitals today?'

'Recovery has been quite rapid, as I told you last night. You're still on a lot of medication. I heard that you wanted to know when you'll be released from hospital?'

I nod.

'Do you want me to be honest?'

'I wouldn't expect anything less from you.'

'Not until the weekend, if it were up to us.'

'But I can leave any time—'

'As a doctor, I wouldn't advise that. You might feel like you're better, but the body needs time to properly heal. And another thing if I may?'

I nod again.

'I strongly recommend you see a therapist. From what I gathered last night, and from whatever little I heard on the local news this morning, you've been through a lot. You might not appreciate it at the moment, and you might think it'll pass, but nothing goes away. The mind subconsciously stores memories and throws them back at you. Please don't take it lightly. See a specialist, they will be able to hold your hand, guide you through this time and it will help you in the long run, trust me.'

There's a thin film of water over my eyes. Everything is blurry, but I'm too proud to raise my hand and wipe away the tears; they roll down my cheeks.

'I'm so sorry something this cruel and wrong happened to someone like you, I truly am, Anushka.'

'Thank you,' I mouth but even I can't hear my voice. He smiles. He's read my lips.

'Aryan, will it be too much to expect to ask you to be present with me when the police arrive? It's just that I've never spoken to the authorities before.' Which is not a lie, but it's not technically correct either. I have spoken to the traffic police more than once. And what about the time the policemen came home for verification after I had applied for my passport after the wedding? But I haven't been part of any real police investigation.

'If you want me to. However, it is up to the police to allow me to sit in on an ongoing investigation.'

'It's just that I am not a hundred per cent myself at the moment, and I don't want to delay meeting the police since my friends told me that my husband is missing. I want to tell the police all the places he could possibly be so that they can find Akbar...' I say, and my voice breaks towards the end.

'I understand that. Let me clear my schedule. And I can request my supervisor, Dr Mehra, to make it clear to the police that they either speak to you with a doctor present, considering your current state, or they can leave it for another day.'

'But I don't want to leave it for another day,' I insist.

'I know, and believe me, neither will the police.' Aryan leaves me, and I realise I forgot to ask him when this IV can be removed. But he'll be back soon and I can check later.

Seven

Two uniformed police officers are ushered into my small hospital room by Aryan, and it suddenly feels crowded. His demeanour suggests that the police have been informed that he will stay with me. Good. From their uniforms and the insignia – the policewoman has two stars adorning her shoulders and is wearing a peaked cap, and the policeman behind has chevrons and wears a khaki beret – it doesn't take my befuddled brain much to establish who's the senior one here. Even going only by their bearing, it is evident who is in charge. Despite my best efforts it's impossible to read the name tags. My eyes simply won't focus.

'Good evening, Mrs Anushka Khan, I'm Assistant Commissioner of Police, Kamala Jha, and this is Constable Bhim Singh.' The constable nods to confirm his greeting. The ACP is young and wears the brass letters 'IPS' alongside the stars on her shoulders. Her job probably keeps her outdoors a lot considering the even tan her face and arms display. She isn't wearing make-up of course – as per the rulebook, it's not permitted in the police force, I know – not even a bindi. She's quite pretty. I bet she's a head-turner when she lets her hair down, with her petite build, the thick leather belt cinching her narrow waist. She has an authoritative face, quick eyes the colour of wet tea leaves, and as she removes her cap, I see that her hair is held up in a sophisticated knot. Stylish. I wonder what I look like at the moment with all the tubes connected to me. I know my face and head hurt, which tells me that there are injuries but how they appear to someone looking at me, I do not know since I haven't had the chance to look at myself in a mirror. I'm certain I look horribly bruised and broken. I wish I could feign an excuse to go to the toilet, but I bet they aren't going to disconnect me from the IV for that; they'll get me a bedpan again instead.

'Hello.' I smile in return. I've already forgotten their names, but I remember her rank: ACP.

'Dr Yadav has informed us that you are willing to give your account to the police – is that correct, Mrs Khan?' ACP certainly knows her job. She's covering all bases in case anyone later accuses her of coercing me into making a statement while declared unfit by the doctor.

I look askance at Aryan. He gives me a near-imperceptible nod, which I pass on to the policewoman. The constable behind her makes a note. Permission asked, answered and recorded, I presume.

'So how're you feeling now, Mrs Khan?'

I can't begin to say how much I've started hating that question in the last twenty-four hours or so.

'Not too bad, all things considered.'

'Firstly, I'm extremely sorry,' the ACP continues, 'having to bother you in the hospital. But I'm sure you are equally keen on finding out what exactly happened at your residence at Sainik Farms...' I can sense derision in her voice by the way she intonates Sainik Farms; it stinks of money, of the privileged class, of all the things most other people will never be able to afford in their lifetimes.

I nod.

'So let me tell you what I have on record here, Mrs Khan—'

'You can call me Anushka.'

'We received a desperate cry for help, logged into the police central system at 23:16. The log reads, "A female resident of Sainik Farms had called 100, the police emergency number, to report a case of domestic abuse." Was that you who called, Mrs Khan?' So she has decided to ignore my request to call me Anushka. Fine.

'Yes.'

'Could you give me an account of the incident and everything that happened, leading up to the point when you made that call to the police, please?'

I look at her, then at Aryan, and then back at her. 'Akbar and I were having a lazy Saturday at home – no guests, no parties to attend that evening. He was fixing drinks for both of us. Gin and tonic for me, bourbon...I think it was Jack Daniel's, for himself.'

'There was no one else in the house at the time? No servants?'

'We usually give them the weekends off to allow ourselves some privacy. Unless we have houseguests over or if we're hosting a party or dinner.'

The ACP nods in agreement. 'What happened next?'

'It must have been around ten-thirty, I'm not sure of the exact time, since I wasn't looking, when we heard a car in our driveway...'

'Don't mind me asking, but there's a closed gate at the end of your long driveway to the main road. How did this person get through the gate without contacting you on the intercom?'

The ACP is sharp. 'We also have a keypad and regular visitors have the code.'

'But that defeats the purpose of a security system, doesn't it?'

'It doesn't because the five-digit code is only shared with close friends,' I explain.

'So, this visitor was a close friend, you say?'

Is she insinuating something? According to the newspaper that Monica brought me, the police recovered Rajiv Pant's corpse from our residence. She knows who the visitor is. Is she asking me to say – to admit – that Rajiv Pant was a close friend? 'Yes,' I say.

'Who was the visitor?'

'Rajiv Pant.'

'And how do you know Rajiv Pant?' *Do*, not *did*. Why is she using the present tense?

'Rajiv Pant was a friend of my husband, Akbar—'

'Was?'

Dr Yadav answered, 'Even I know the body found at Anushka's residence was Rajiv Pant's, madam. It's all over the news.'

Thank you, Aryan, I want to say.

'Oh, I wasn't aware Anushka had access to the news here in the hospital.' She's sharp, this one. She's now close enough for me to read her name tag: Kamala Jha. 'Please continue.'

'Akbar, like I mentioned, was quite drunk – so was I – and when he saw Rajiv at our doorstep, he went ballistic.'

'Why?'

'Akbar wrongly believed that Rajiv was having some kind of an affair with me.' I feel ashamed voicing it.

'Mrs Khan, what is "some kind of an affair" really? Did your husband suspect you of having an affair with Rajiv or not?'

'He suspected us of having an extramarital affair.'

'Was it true?'

'Was what true?' I know exactly what she's asking, but suddenly I have the impulse to fight this woman's accusations. And moreover, she said it so calmly, as if she were asking whether I was having coffee with a neighbour.

'Were you having an extramarital affair with Rajiv Pant?'

'No. Rajiv was Akbar's friend. I haven't the foggiest idea why Akbar ever imagined me having an affair with Rajiv or anyone else for that matter.'

'OK. So what happened when Akbar saw Rajiv?'

'I was in the living room, and I heard shouting in the entrance foyer.'

'What were they saying?'

'I couldn't catch any words.'

'I've been in your house, Mrs Khan. While the foyer is not visible from the living room, it's not so distant that you can't hear the words.' She says it without any emotion, but her tone is challenging me.

'You have to understand that I was drunk. And scared – I knew Akbar had a temper, and seeing Rajiv at our doorstep when we were having a quiet evening in...he flared up just as I had feared. So maybe I retreated into myself, wondering what to do next.'

'What happened then?'

'As I walked out of the living room into the foyer, I saw Akbar holding the gun. Only then did I hear his words.'

'What was he saying?'

'I don't remember the exact words but something like, "*I'll kill both of you. I'll shoot you first and then shoot the bitch...*"' I can't carry on any further, I break down. Aryan rushes to me, takes my right hand in his and checks my pulse.

'Could we have a five-minute break please?' he asks.

'Yes, of course. Constable Bhim Singh, could you get coffee for both of us please?'

'I'll arrange that.' Aryan walks out the door.

Eight

'Mrs Khan, your call to the police emergency helpline was prioritised since the officer who took it told us you were slurring, your words were punctuated with sobs. And so, sensing the imminent danger to your life, he passed on the call to the nearest police chowki, which is in Sainik Farms…' the policewoman is telling us now.

The ACP and the constable drank the coffee Aryan ordered for them while I told them about the incident, picking up from the moment I saw Akbar holding the gun. He had grabbed my neck from behind and had pushed me hard. I fell on the console table in the foyer, and my head hit the mirror on the wall. He came after me, but I remember how he was pulled back by Rajiv. I took the opportunity to escape his clutches and ran into the bedroom, locking it from the inside. I was drunk, I was scared, and I fell yet again. I heard a shot a few minutes later. I also told her that Akbar was banging on the bedroom door as I made that call to the police. At the time, I had no idea that he had shot Rajiv dead in our house. I had imagined that he had fired into the air, warning Rajiv to leave immediately. ACP Kamala Jha thought it put things into perspective. It was likely that the moment Akbar realised I was on a call to the police, he knew time was running out.

He had to do something. He couldn't make me open the door, so he did the next best thing he could: he bolted from the scene. It made sense, or at least that was the impression she gave us.

'Sainik Farms…' ACP Jha's voice breaks my train of thought. '…is a very small outfit, and so they called us at the Saket Police Station for assistance. Sainik Farms isn't in our jurisdiction but since the case was assigned to me, I organised the force and approached with lights and sirens on. We must have got there around midnight?' She turns and looks at the constable who turns pages in his notebook and responds.

'Yes, madam-jee.'

'Thankfully, the Sainik Farms police had called for an ambulance, which was already there. When we got there they were loading you into the van to bring you here.'

'Anushka's quite lucky she got here when she did. If there had been any delay, it might have been difficult to revive her,' Aryan offers, unsolicited.

'Were you here when she was brought in?'

'No, but I've seen the file.'

'What exactly was her state when she was brought in?'

'She was bleeding, her forehead was cut open, which required five sutures. She was drunk and overdosed on sleeping pills—'

'Sleeping pills? Who gave you the sleeping pills?' ACP Jha asks me.

'I don't know. I didn't take them.'

'You think your husband mixed the pills in your drinks?'

'Like I said, I don't know. I couldn't taste any difference.'

'Anushka is correct, if you mix one or two tablets into alcohol with a mixer as strong as tonic water, there is little chance that the drinker will notice the difference.'

ACP Jha nods as if she agrees, but I can see she's a little annoyed by Aryan interjecting. 'How many drinks do you think you had, Mrs Khan?' she asks.

'Oh, I can't tell you. I mean…we started drinking around four or five—'

'Is that typical? You and your husband start drinking at that time in the evening?'

Is she judging us for drinking cocktails in our own house? 'Not typical, but not something we hadn't done before. We'd done this several times before when we were home over the weekend. We would drink until late, then call for food delivery, and maybe catch a film on Netflix later before calling it a day.'

'Hmm...' The *hmm* sounds judgemental. ACP Jha certainly doesn't subscribe to this imprudent, extravagant life. 'So, if we were to estimate, you might have had five or six drinks in those five to six hours?'

'I'd double that estimate. I don't take an hour to finish a drink.'

'Seven or more, then.' I think I read the words 'irresponsible' or 'harlot' on her lips, but she doesn't let them out.

'Hmm...seven drinks. If we take our good doctor's opinion...' she gestures towards Aryan, '...you could have consumed up to ten sleeping tablets too?'

'I don't think so,' Aryan intervenes again. 'If Mr Akbar Khan started feeding her the tablets from the first drink onwards, Anushka would have passed out a lot earlier.'

'So what are you saying?'

'I think Mr Khan started mixing Anushka's drinks later after she had had a few drinks already.'

'Either way,' ACP Jha dismisses the finer details and addresses me. 'If your husband was giving you sleeping pills, he had already decided to do something ominous. To you or to your friend, which could well mean that he premeditated this.'

'I can't believe Akbar would plan such a thing.'

'Why not? If, as you say, he thought you were having an affair with his friend, it doesn't take too much of a leap to guess at what he was doing and why.'

'But how was Akbar to know Rajiv would be coming to see us that evening?'

'That one is easy to answer. He called him.' ACP Jha says it without any change in her tone. A bland, matter-of-fact statement.

'Who called whom?'

'Your husband, Akbar Khan, called Rajiv Pant.'

'Why would he call Rajiv?'

'You tell me.'

'I don't know.'

'Well, then we'll only find out once we find Akbar.'

'Wait a minute…how do you know Akbar called Rajiv?' I ask. I can see Aryan is equally involved in the story by now.

'Because we found his phone.'

'You found Akbar's phone? Where?'

'Your husband left his phone at home. He knew we would be able to track him down using his GPS coordinates.'

'Oh that's why—'

'What?'

'I had a friend over earlier today. She told me she's been leaving messages for him on his phone, but never received a call back. So the phone is with the police.'

'Yes, we have his phone and also Rajiv's phone. A call was made to Rajiv's number at around ten that evening. If you two were together the entire evening, how come you didn't know about that?'

'I didn't. It must have been when I went to the toilet or when he went to relieve himself. Or when he went to fix a drink for me near the bar.'

'How long did this call last?' Aryan asks a good question.

'Less than two minutes.'

'He certainly made it when he was out of my earshot then.'

'Is there anything else you'd like to tell us, Mrs Khan?'

'About?'

'About anything, about yourself or the Saturday evening in question, particularly…'

'I'm trying to wrap my head around what you've just told me. That my husband might have been mixing sleeping tablets in my drinks before calling his friend. That this wasn't a spur-of-the-moment flare-up of some sort where Akbar lost control, that he had planned to kill both of us.'

'It looks like that, and the time frame fits. He started feeding you pills from say 9 p.m. onwards. If our good doctor's assessment is correct and he gave you two pills per drink, you had roughly eight to ten pills in your system by the time Rajiv arrived at your door. So yes, I'd say he had planned it all.'

'I cannot believe it.'

'Well, we will leave you for now. I can see you're tired. We have your husband's car details, and we know of the two other places he owns. We've called both of them and he hasn't arrived at either. Not yet anyway. We have put his photograph on the wanted list, so it would be difficult for him to check into a hotel too – at least, not any that ask for identification, so unless he's hiding with some friend and decides to stay indoors for a long, long time, I'm sure we'll find him very soon, don't worry.'

'What if he comes here?' I ask. 'It's most likely he will want to finish what he started, isn't it?'

'I doubt he'll take that risk, but I'm sure we can arrange security for a few days.'

I nod my acquiescence.

'And if you remember anything that you think may help in our inquiry, please call us immediately.' ACP Kamala Jha takes out her card and places it on the table at my bedside. 'This is my mobile number.'

'Thank you.'

'You take care.'

I look at my best friend, the clock on the wall. It is nearly six in the evening. Some of my senses are working now, despite the sedatives, which Aryan, my second-best friend at the moment, tells me have all but left my body by now. I am my natural self now except for the injuries and those will take a little while to heal. The scar where they stitched me up on my forehead will heal into a light mark not thicker than a line, and my second-best friend also tells me that if I am willing to pay, they can get a plastic surgeon to cover that up too. Not something to worry about at all. And that can be done within months of my getting back to my life. They cannot do it at the moment since the wound is a little raw, whatever that means.

I close my eyes. I can hear the door moan as Aryan leaves. Having ascertained I am alone, I open my eyes. It is then that I finally cry. It isn't so much the pain but the uncertainty. What's going to happen now? Ironically, even those who make meticulous plans over a long time are known to stumble and fail. And me, I don't even have a plan. Akbar has been a part of my life for so long that I don't know how I'll move forward. This is all so devastating.

I close my eyes again and let myself slip into sleep.

TUESDAY, 9TH JULY

Nine

'How have you been, Anush?' Aanya drops by in the morning with her husband, Siddharth Dhariwal, a.k.a. Sid. I know the couple well. They are Akbar's friends too, going back to before I moved to Delhi. Now we're mutual friends. The two look very much alike, like siblings. Both are regulars at the gym and are extremely well-maintained and groomed. Sid has one of those chiselled bodies that one associates with runway models or Hrithik Roshan, and she'd score a perfect ten in any bikini contest. Both of them are good-looking too. Made for each other, you might think – well they are and they are not. Theirs is a very peculiar relationship, although most people in our social circle aren't aware of it. Aanya confided in me, when drunk, quite early on after we met. Sid knows that I know, but he told me not to share it with Akbar, that the two live separate lives under a shared roof. They love each other, no doubt about it, but they got married very early – right out of school, Aanya told me. Their alliance was apparently fixed when they were born, a business partnership consolidated between families by promising their children to each other. They have been friends since their childhood – but both of them are gay. She has her partners and he has his. Don't ask, don't tell. They are comfortable with their arrangement, so why should anyone care? Or intervene? The parents think it's a happy marriage. Aanya gets harangued by both her mother and mother-in-law to have kids soon since they've been married for over a decade now, but Aanya and Sid aren't inclined to oblige their parents to that extent. The parents, it seems, are pathetically clinging to their fantasy, and have no idea that the marriage hasn't been consummated. But the two are best friends, confidants, and great partners in life and, now, in business.

'I'm really sorry but I have to ask. I'm kind of desperate to know where Akbar is. Is he living with you?' I ask urgently, after I've assured them I'm fine and narrated to them what I've learned from Monica and Piyush, Dr Aryan, and the police.

Both of them look at each other strangely. They think I'm crazy. Maybe I am.

'Trust me, Akbar isn't with us,' Sid says. 'No one we've spoken to knows where he is. I guess whatever happened at your place on Saturday night happened in a fit of rage and madness, and maybe he came to his senses immediately afterwards. I do not think he had a plan for where he would go after—'

'I thought so too, Sid, but I no longer think that is the case. The evidence suggests that it was all intentional, at least on his part. He might have mixed sleeping pills in my drinks. The police say he called Rajiv from his phone. I'm guessing he called Rajiv to invite him over to our house so how could it be unplanned or unprepared?'

Aanya is holding my hand. She gives it a gentle squeeze, purses her lips and gives me an empathetic nod.

'The doctor told me that if I had been given another three or four tablets, or if there had been any delay in my getting to the hospital, it could have been fatal. They had to pump my stomach to get all that out. I'm sure he had every intention to finish me. I just don't know if he had planned to take Rajiv out too.'

'Why did he suspect you and Rajiv of having an affair?'

'I don't know how his warped mind works.'

'He was getting a bit kinky over the last couple of months, I have to admit,' Sid shrugs.

Both Aanya and I look at Sid. 'How do you mean?' I ask.

'He sent me photographs of you in rather sexy lingerie, and although you looked stunning, Akbar doesn't know that I have no interest in women...'

'What?'

'Why didn't you tell me?' Aanya asks.

'I didn't think it was important enough. I honestly thought he had sent them to me by mistake, instead of...'

'Instead of?' I am hysterical.

'Look,' Sid is sheepish now. 'Akbar told me, in confidence, that he suspected Rajiv and you were having an affair; there's little point in me concealing that. So, in my daft brain, I thought he had meant to send those photographs to Rajiv to demonstrate that you were two-timing Rajiv by having sex with them both...I'm really sorry.'

'How could you believe him?' Aanya is aghast.

'I'm not saying I believed him but as his friend, if he told me something, I had to be discreet. I wouldn't go around telling everyone, would I?'

'I'm not everyone. I am at least your legally wedded wife.'

'I know, and I said I'm sorry. Anush, I'm really sorry. I should've told him off, but I didn't.'

'Where are those photographs?' I ask.

'I deleted them, I swear.'

'Do you have any idea if he sent them to anyone else?'

'We never spoke about them. Like I said, I believed he had mistakenly sent them to me – maybe he was drunk, I don't know – but we never spoke about them.'

'I can't believe it. Akbar used to take photographs of me sometimes, but I had no idea he had a motive behind that too.'

'You never truly know someone.' Wise words from Sid.

'Well, this corroborates the police's hypothesis that the events of Saturday night were orchestrated, and not improvised.'

'Of course, why else has he gone missing?' I don't know if I should cry or seethe in anger.

'It makes sense for him to take flight under the circumstances. He'll be charged with cold-blooded murder and additionally – considering the amount of drugs the doctor flushed out of your body – with attempted murder, when the police apprehend him.'

'But...where could he go?' I ask Sid.

'I honestly can't tell you.'

'Are you sure you're not hiding anything more from us?' Aanya asks him.

'I swear to God, I'm not. Not now after I know all this. And you came with me, you've seen the crime scene and although friends aren't supposed to take sides against each other, I am with Anush on this one.'

'I thought our house was cordoned off by the police and no one was allowed in. How did you manage to get inside my house?' It shouldn't surprise me though. Sid's family has political connections. I'm sure he called one of the ministers who called a top-ranking cop and arranged the visit.

'We were allowed in. We wore those white-paper clothes and gloves. We were told not to touch anything, and there was a policewala with us the entire time we were inside the house so we wouldn't contaminate or eliminate any evidence…'

'It's not like we even knew what would or wouldn't make it as evidence in the case,' Aanya adds.

'They had taken Rajiv's body away, but the amount of blood still on the floor was enough to know what had occurred there. The large mirror over your console table in the entrance foyer was smashed too. I'm so, so sorry, Anush. I wish I had known that Akbar is such a tyrant…'

I break into sobs.

***

'I guess I've never understood what motivates people to do strange things,' Aryan declares that afternoon, after I tell him about the visit from Aanya and Sid.

'How do you mean?'

'Don't get me wrong, but I can't imagine what kind of fascination or morbid curiosity your friends possess that compelled them to visit the crime scene while the investigation is ongoing.' Aryan is clearly surprised. 'I mean, would you rush to see a place like that?'

'I wouldn't, but Aanya and Sid are different in a lot of ways. They can pull strings to get in anywhere and this might've been just one phone call.'

'If I had that kind of connection and influence, I'd get the top floor of the Qutub Minar opened and spend an evening sipping champagne there. Or ask for permission to spend a night in the Taj Mahal, not go and see a crime scene where my friend has murdered another friend, and beaten up his wife...I'm sorry, I didn't mean to...'

'It's OK. What you're saying isn't wrong. Sometimes, I wonder what made me stay and endure for such a long time, but it's not like life offered me several choices to pick from. It was either staying married to Akbar or...what actually? My parents are dead, I am penniless, and all my friends are his friends. Where would I go? What would I do? I am just a graduate; I didn't sit for the bar exam. What job could I possibly find in Delhi with no experience whatsoever? A waitress? A salesgirl? How would I survive in this city?'

'I understand, Anushka. I totally understand. While people think it's always a question of choices we make, what they forget is that those choices are limited. It may be that the choices were in the past—'

'Like not getting married to Akbar, and studying further, I know. But there are so many of my classmates who studied further and got nowhere. You're correct, I could have been lucky. But I was filled with the feeling shared by my family that I had struck gold – I felt so lucky that an erstwhile nawab, with more inheritance than most people's earnings over an entire lifetime, had already proposed marriage to me. How could I have declined that stroke of luck to look for another? You see what I mean?'

'Completely. I come from a lower-middle-class family too, don't forget. You get an opportunity like that you jump, you don't decline it to jump later.'

'But where does it leave me now?'

'Who inherits everything if Akbar is arrested?'

'I don't know…wait a minute…are you insinuating that I made Akbar murder his friend to get him incarcerated for life so I can inherit his wealth?' My voice rises an octave.

'Not in the least. I'm only trying to think like the police.'

'But Akbar is missing. The wife of a missing person does not inherit anything as far as I know. And even when he is arrested, if he is sentenced to life imprisonment, it's not like he's mentally unstable and can't write a will. If he believed I was straying, why would he bequeath anything to me? I'll be a pauper again. At least, I have friends in Delhi now, and I have lived a life I hadn't even dreamt of growing up. So no grudges or complaints, honestly.'

'Really?'

'I'll ask for a divorce as soon as I get out of the hospital. I don't know if it can be granted in absentia, but I'll look up my options when I get out.'

'All I can do is wish you luck, Anushka. It's been a revelation meeting someone like you.'

'It's so nice of you to say that, Aryan. Same here. I wish we had met under different circumstances.'

'Your circumstances will change when you get out of here and get a divorce. We can always meet again.'

I smile at him. He's a nice guy, I can tell.

'I think you should rest now. I was informed that the police will come again tomorrow. They have some more questions, so I've requested that they come over after 2 p.m. when I'm here. I'm sorry I didn't consult you but I assumed you'd want me around.'

'You didn't have to do that, I'm a lot better now. The initial shock has worn off, and I can handle them.'

'It's no bother at all. I want to be there.'

'Thank you,' I say.

'I'll leave you now, I think you should rest.'

'I think so too.'

Ten

My best friend on the wall tells me it is ten minutes past ten. If it were an analogue clock, this would be the ideal clock-face most advertisements for timepieces are shot at. I have enough sense now to figure out it's night-time, and not the next morning. I haven't catnapped for so long, then. I notice that my left hand is a bit free. While the cannula is still taped to the veins in the back of my hand, the tube has been detached. That's a good sign. Maybe I could get something to eat. Biryani?

What I get instead is a visitor, and someone I least expect.

Kamala Jha walks into my room without warning, unaccompanied. Yes, it is ACP Kamala Jha, albeit without her constable or uniform.

She's wearing a white polo-neck T-shirt and skinny-fit jeans, which show off her petite frame.

'Hello.'

'Hi,' I respond in greeting. Didn't Aryan say the police would only visit me again tomorrow when he was around?

'I thought we could have a little chat.' Kamala comes closer and sits on the only chair in the room, next to my bed.

'Of course,' I say, knowing all too well that a policewoman, on her own, in my hospital room at this hour, isn't here for a friendly chat. Far from it. She has a definite agenda. The police are not your foe, but they never are your friends either.

'How're you feeling?'

The question is too much now. 'I'm a lot better. What brings you here at this hour? I was told you'd be coming to see me tomorrow afternoon?'

'Of course, I'll come tomorrow afternoon. But that will be as a police officer.'

And what precisely are you here as now? I want to ask but I don't. They're not foes but I don't have to make enemies of them either. I smile at her but I have no idea what she's here for.

'I wanted to ask you some questions, which I thought might feel awkward for you with the constable around...and your doctor friend,' she adds.

'You mean Dr Yadav.'

'Aryan, as you call him.' She is nothing if not observant. I don't have any opinion on how she perceives my relationship with Aryan. He's good-looking. He's hinted at meeting me later. When, how, where – and if it's even going to happen for real? He could be saying that to a lot of patients, for all I know.

'Yes, we chatted an entire evening, he was considerate, so we became friends and are now on a first-name basis.'

'I'm not here to judge.'

'There's nothing here for you to judge.' I'm peeved by her attitude. 'So what brings you here?'

'Good question. OK, I'm technically not here to discuss the ongoing murder investigation. But I won't lie. I'm here because I want some background context. I'm here because if I cannot establish a motive, it's impossible to put things into a frame. It might help me find your husband.'

'OK...what do you want from me?'

'Were you having an affair with Rajiv Pant?'

I study Kamala's face. She's pretty. Prettier than she seems to give herself credit for. In mufti, off-duty, she has some make-up on, her hair is in a ponytail, her thin and long neck exposed – reminding me how Akbar liked and hated mine, all at the same time. I appreciate that her informal chat is about knowing the truth. She might be struggling to crack this case, she needs something to cling to or else why would she be here, after hours, to talk to me? She's here on a definitive mission.

'What's that got to do with where Akbar is now?'

'Trust me, at this stage neither you nor I know what has a bearing on the investigation and what doesn't. So, could you tell me if you and Rajiv were having an affair and if you suspect that it led to his death?'

'No. Rajiv and I weren't having an affair. We were friends, like I told you. I enjoyed his company, and that's it.'

'So, if I were to go ahead and ask you for your fingerprints to compare with any unknown ones we recover from Rajiv's car, we wouldn't find any match with yours, correct?'

'Well, I didn't say I never sat in his car.' Where is this policewoman going with this? She's not in uniform, she said she's not here in her official capacity either. Can I stop her from asking any further questions?

'Of course, you didn't. What about his house?'

'I've been there. Like all his other friends, Akbar and I have been to his house a million times over the years.'

'And his bedroom? What about your fingerprints in his bedroom? On the headboard or the side rails? Do you think he took all his friends into his bedroom?'

'What are you implying?'

She looks at me intently, waiting for me to continue. 'Please don't lie to me.'

'OK, I wasn't strictly having an affair with Rajiv. We did sleep together a few times, but that's it.'

'More than a few times, I believe, but, like I said, I'm not here to judge.'

'It's funny that you say you don't judge, but you've mentioned how you're *not judging* me twice, unsolicited, in the past few minutes.'

'I'm sorry if I've offended you, it wasn't my intention,' she says it compassionately. I nod.

'How do you think your husband came to know that you and Rajiv Pant met secretly?'

'I have no idea.'

'I do. Your car had a GPS tracker installed. Someone was monitoring your movements, and I cannot think of anyone else who would gain anything from doing so.'

'Oh my God, you think Akbar...?'

'Either he put it there himself or, most likely, he asked a private investigator to put a tail on you, since I cannot find anything on his phone or computer that tells me if he received any data from that device.'

'But if he engaged a private investigator, there might be a chain of emails or phone records?'

'Nothing. He might have another phone, unlisted. That's probably why he left his phone at home when he left on Saturday night. He knows that it will be impossible for the police to track him down without it.'

'GPS device, private investigator…if he had been collecting evidence against me, why did he have to wait so long to confront me? And why get Rajiv to come to our place that evening?'

'I share your confusion. He could have just as easily gone to Rajiv's house and shot him there and made it look like a burglary gone wrong. Or he could have hired someone to do that and then distanced himself from it. He had no lack of money. Then, on a later day, you could have succumbed to a drug overdose. Although the police aren't so dumb that we might not have connected the two unnatural deaths, there was always a chance it could go unnoticed if the case didn't make it to the media, or wasn't attended to by two separate police stations, which is most likely since you live in Delhi and Rajiv lived in Gurgaon.'

I don't know what to say.

'But I can also understand the passion, the hurt, the fact that your husband was drunk, out of his senses, and that things got a bit out of control.'

'Didn't you say Akbar made a call to Rajiv that evening?'

'Yes he did, but your husband might have called Rajiv for a chat. Perhaps he was provoked, maybe he felt threatened by Rajiv and acted in self-defence…perhaps Akbar Khan hadn't premeditated it after all, which makes it culpable homicide of the third degree, and which carries the lowest punishment under the law.'

'What about the fact that Akbar pulled out his gun?'

'There are no witnesses to the haadsaa except you. Maybe Rajiv Pant brought the gun to the scene? The gun isn't licensed, it's from the black market. It could be anyone's.'

'But I told you in the presence of Dr Aryan and the constable that I saw Akbar go to the study to get his gun—'

'Under the circumstances, *you* – having been under the influence of drugs and alcohol, as your doctor friend told us – are not the most reliable witness. You could have made a mistake…'

I blink. I can't follow what she's saying. Why is she trying to protect Akbar?

'ACP Jha—'

'Call me Kamala for now.'

'Kamala, you're almost speaking in tongues here. What's your motive for reducing a murder charge in the first degree to the third?'

'Well, Akbar doesn't have to stay hidden. Currently, he likely thinks he's going to get arrested for a premeditated murder and go in for a long time. If he were to know that his actions carry a reduced charge he might be inclined to give himself up, don't you think?'

Aha! The penny eventually drops. 'Do you think I know where Akbar is?'

'I didn't say that, but the thought has crossed my mind if I'm being honest.'

'So that's why you're visiting me after hours without the constable or anyone else present so you can impress upon me that you're on my side?'

'I *am* on your side, can't you see? Akbar can come home, and he'll get a short sentence if you support him at the trial—'

'So you want me to call Akbar and ask him to return?'

'I think that is very much in your interest too.'

'But I don't know where he is!'

'So you say…' Kamala says, and I can sense the sarcasm in her tone now.

'I genuinely don't know.'

'Let me ask you this: has your husband ever left home without his phone? Like, ever?'

'He doesn't even go to the toilet without it.'

'Do you think he was kidnapped?'

'No. Who would kidnap my husband? It's too far-fetched to even consider that someone killed Rajiv and kidnapped Akbar on the same night.'

'Precisely. I mean if you, like me, don't think he was kidnapped after the murder, what is the probability of him accidentally dropping his phone along with the gun at the crime scene and somehow disappearing?'

'Next to zero, almost.'

'Exactly. So he's certainly carrying a phone to be in touch with someone, correct?'

'Possibly, but he's not been in touch with me, I swear.'

'You want me to trust you, but you also lied about having an affair with the deceased, Rajiv Pant. And then immediately did a one-eighty turn when I challenged your story with evidence. At the moment, I don't have any evidence that you're in touch with Akbar, but perhaps it's a matter of time. I will find it, believe me. You can save me the time, and save yourself a prison sentence by cooperating with the police. In return, I promise to keep this conversation a secret, and you have my word that I'll help Akbar get the least possible sentence. It's not a bad deal. Think about it.'

'I'm sorry, I'm really tired now.' I close my eyes. I don't want to entertain her any more.

I want her gone without antagonising her by asking her to get lost.

'I'll be back tomorrow afternoon to take your statement again.'

I can sense her presence in the room with my eyes closed for a while. I hear the door creak softly. She's gone. I lie there, thinking about her visit. Her true agenda for this late-night visit has become apparent. First, she put me on the back foot and threw a googly to make me admit having an affair with Rajiv. Then she proposed that I change my testimony in the absence of any witnesses. She had planned it well. She wanted me to believe she was a friend but I knew she was not. She's devious. She was here suggesting I know where Akbar is. Crafty. I know that in law it would amount to what they call *aiding and abetting after the fact*. I'm not falling for her bait.

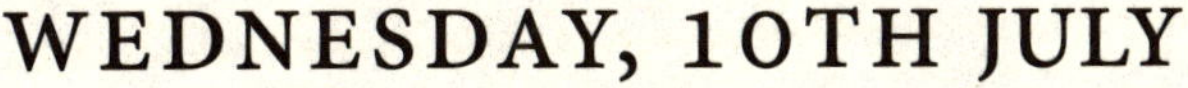

WEDNESDAY, 10TH JULY

Eleven

I don't remember when I drifted off to sleep, but I remember shutting my eyes to let the policewoman know that I was no longer interested in talking to her. But this morning, I woke up around eight-thirty, and I feel fresh. There's some pain in my forehead, and my neck still hurts, but I know the doctor will change my dressing and check on the sutures during his rounds. I am guessing I will be out of the hospital by the weekend.

The conversation with ACP Kamala Jha reverberates in my mind. What gave her the idea that Akbar might be in touch with me? And how can he be? The police have taken away my phone. I do not have a secret, unregistered phone stashed in the hospital room.

'Good morning.' Cynthia's smiling face appears in the room. Thank God. My thoughts were scary and depressive.

'Good morning, Cynthia.' Her demeanour makes it apparent that I've responded a tad more enthusiastically than she expected.

'You seem to be in good spirits, ma'am.'

'Anushka.' Why do they all make it sound so formal?

'Sorry. Anushka. Did you sleep well?'

'Like a toddler.'

'That's really good to know. I'm so happy for you,' she says, but something is off.

'What's wrong, Cynthia?'

'Somehow...your...recovery feels like a personal victory. I'm sorry.' She's almost in tears, her voice choking.

I know all too well that I am hardly in any condition to ease anyone else's miseries or life problems, especially considering the situation I am presently in. But I can't bear to see another human so sad in my presence. 'You want to talk about it?'

'No, it's against the rules...'

'Rules? Rules should never keep us from telling the truth.' Big words coming from someone in my situation.

'It's…' She turns to look at the door to see if it's shut. I gesture towards the camera – I had seen Aryan switch it off before he broke the rules – and she acts instantaneously. She switches it off. It would only be much, much later in life that I would come to know that any patient, in any hospital is well within their human rights to ask the nurse or doctor or any employee of the hospital to switch off the camera placed in their room for monitoring. Everyone – however undeserving they are – has a right to privacy. Which also reminds me that my last night's tête-à-tête with Kamala might have been recorded. I bet she doesn't know there was a camera. Was it recorded? Should I ask Cynthia or wait for Aryan? I decide on the latter. The camera either records or it doesn't. If it does I assume the recording is kept for twenty-four hours at least, or else what's the point?

'You were saying something,' I prompt Cynthia.

'I'm a victim of domestic violence too.' She breaks down, and I feel bad. 'I thought it was a malady of the poor. I had no idea such practices of abuse existed in the upper class, I'm sorry…' Tears are now gushing out of her eyes. I can see her pain, the agony. And I can appreciate her point of view. If I – an upper-class, rich, educated woman, married to an erstwhile nawab – have to be brought in by ambulance after being badly injured by my husband, what more can she expect? There's no utopia left in her mind to imagine now, is there? No amount of education, no money, no social life shields you from domestic abuse. In her sad, mournful eyes, I can see hopes and wishes crumbling.

'Each case is unalike, everyone has a different story, Cynthia. We mustn't lose heart. It doesn't happen in every household, so you don't have to look at it like all women are doomed to experience abuse.'

'I know, but—'

'Stop the ifs and buts, we are better than this. If your husband is abusive, talk to him. Call him out when you are with your parents or his, or when you have friends over. Explain that he cannot get away with abusing you, his wife. You are an independent woman, you need to live without fear. If he loves you, he'll understand. If he doesn't, you need to make some hard decisions. Kick him out…'

'You know how difficult it is for a single woman to survive in this city, Anushka didi.' She cannot help adding the didi and I don't correct her.

'I know, and that's the challenge, Cynthia. We either accept our fate or we make the decision to walk away and take up the challenge of being single – less money, but it's about liberation, about independence – the choice is ours, isn't it?'

'If your husband returned, would you take him back?'

Her question throws me off guard.

It's one thing to advise others on their problems; it's a completely different ballgame when you are in exactly the same situation. If anything this girl has inadvertently firmed up my resolve. I am not cowering for Kamala, I'm not lying so that this world can believe Akbar isn't absconding, and that I know where he is. I am *not* going to say my husband acted in self-defence. I feel stupid that I was gullible enough to have trusted the ACP by acknowledging that I had an affair with Rajiv. Yes, I had sex with another man. It might be a sin, but it's not a crime. I cannot take it back now. But that does not, in any way, shape or form, declare that I'm colluding with Akbar. I know I am not colluding with anyone.

'No,' I respond to her question with as much confidence as I can muster. 'No,' I repeat.

'I will take your counsel, didi, and speak to Lalit, my husband.'

'Why don't you try to convince him to come here, and we'll talk to him together?'

'Really? Would you talk to him?'

'Of course.'

Cynthia's face lights up. She flashes me a 440-watt smile. Even if it hurts me I give her a big smile back. Woman to woman. The ACP was lying through and through. This, on the other hand, is real.

'Can I ask you something, Cynthia?'

'Yes please.' She is eager to please now.

‘This camera.’ I point towards the plug she had switched off before we delved into a personal conversation. ‘Does it record or is it just for monitoring?’

‘It records, didi. If something goes wrong, the hospital authorities can look at the events of the past twenty-four hours to evaluate. It saves us from a lot of *he-said-she-said* legal problems. Also, it shows if the patient was attended to at allocated times. And also, when required, we can rush to assist.’

‘So you keep the recording for twenty-four hours?’

‘It’s in a loop. When the disc it is recording over gets full, and if no one needs to retrieve that particular day’s events, then the software starts overwriting it. I know that because Lalit works in another hospital, and he’s one of the staff there working round the clock to maintain the equipment. I used to work there too before I moved jobs, to this hospital.’

‘OK.’ So much for the ACP visiting in the middle of the night to avoid any witnesses.

Cynthia asks me what I would like for a light breakfast and I request two soft-boiled eggs and a buttered wholemeal toast.

Twelve

I break down when Aanya and Sid visit me again in the morning. I hesitate to tell them about the surreptitious nocturnal visit by ACP Kamala Jha. I cannot tell them the true motive behind her visit without revealing my affair with Rajiv. But the more I think about it, the more logical it seems to have friends on my side, should the ACP try to railroad me yet again. Sid has political influence. He will certainly make a better chaperone than Aryan when Kamala visits me this afternoon.

I tell them all. I tell them about my brief sexual affair with Rajiv without divulging much. I can see it surprises them, but they aren’t put off. I tell them that Kamala implied I knew where Akbar was, and that I was keeping his current location from the police, which amounts to a crime. I also mention her hinting at reducing the charges against Akbar if I help her entrap him.

Sid is aghast. 'She broke protocol by simply coming over without explicit permission from the hospital authorities. You are still under the doctor's care and have not yet been signed out of the hospital by them, but I can see her motivation. She's trying all possible tactics to find Akbar.'

'Have you spoken to any other friends? Does anyone know where Akbar is?' I ask.

'Trust me, I've called as many people as I could and checked, but no one has any idea where he's gone.'

'Have they checked if his passport is at home?'

'I assume the police must have checked that. At any rate, the police arrived at your house within, what twenty to thirty minutes of your call? They must have alerted the airports and unless Akbar has a fake one, he couldn't have passed immigration in any event, I suppose.'

'Nonetheless, could you check if it is at home? We might know more about his intentions when he left the other night. Both our passports should be in his study.'

'I'll take care of it, I'll go round personally and check that today itself.'

'You must think I'm a slut.' I never expected people in our friend circle to find out about Rajiv and me, but it was inevitable after his murder, I think. It had to come out, it might make the news.

'Who a person sleeps with is not anyone's business, Anush,' Aanya says. 'And we aren't Draconian. On the contrary, we are the last people to judge anyone given our relationship, and you know that. I can see how Akbar might have reacted violently, but the police shouldn't use that to shame you or coerce you into doing something illegal.' Sid is firm.

'She's going to be back to interrogate me again at two today.' I look at the clock. It's almost noon now. 'And to be honest, I'm terrified.'

'You want us to stay with you when she comes?' Aanya asks.

'I doubt she will let you stay when she questions me. She was quite fussy that I had asked the doctor to stay with me in the room the last time she was here.'

'She cannot stop you from having a friend around unless she thinks you're a suspect. If she suspects you of concealing information about Akbar's whereabouts – what can she possibly do? She can't arrest you and march you down to the police station until the hospital formally releases you from their care. If I even remotely sense she's playing you, I promise I'll step in, stop her questions and we'll get the best lawyer for you.'

'Thank you.'

'I think it might be a bit too overwhelming if both of us remain here, so maybe I'll stay and Aanya can go around to your house to check the passports in the meantime. That is, if the police haven't already found them yet,' Sid suggests.

'Thank you,' I say again.

'I still cannot believe the ACP called on you unannounced at such an unearthly hour.'

'I think her visit has been captured on the camera which was operational when she came into my room last night.' I point towards it. 'I was waiting to confirm if there is a recording of our conversation when the doctor arrives today.'

'Brilliant. I know someone high up in the management team here. I'll call and check. If we have that ACP on camera, then she'd better be careful when she comes to see you today.' Sid is all riled up.

'Really?' That is news to me. 'We should certainly secure a copy of the video then.'

'Give me a few minutes,' Sid says and steps out of the room to make a call.

He returns after a few minutes with a smile on his face. 'I've asked them to get a copy made and send it across to me as soon as possible. I also called someone to let us know if the police had collected Akbar's passport. They'll get back to me soon.'

'Thanks.'

***

Aryan arrives on the dot at two. He checks my vitals and asks if I've had my first meal yet. I introduce him to Aanya and Sid.

'Good to meet you both,' he says politely. Then to me: 'Do you still want me to be here when the ACP comes to talk to you this afternoon?'

'No, thank you.'

'Oh, she's already been here last night, trying to intimidate Anush, so I'm waiting for her to come in. I'll be here with Anush, don't you worry,' Sid tells him.

'Really? I don't think she signed in when she visited you last night.'

'She decided to just "drop by" for a chat.' Sid gives him a summary of what I narrated to him just a while ago, omitting the details of my affair.

'That's absolutely unacceptable. What's the point of having rules if the police themselves break them?' Aryan looks annoyed. 'Such surprise visits aren't ideal for a patient's convalescence, especially someone like Anushka, who's been in a serious and traumatic situation. You need time to heal, and not be continuously forced to relive the events over and over again. I understand that the police want to find Mr Akbar Khan, but they must be considerate towards the victim too.'

'Thank you for caring, Aryan,' I assuage him. 'You've been a great help.'

'It's the least I could do, Anushka.'

'Thank you for looking after our friend so well, Doctor,' Aanya adds.

'How do you want to handle this?' Sid asks when Aryan is gone.

'I don't know.'

'Then leave it to me.' I like the way Sid has taken it upon himself to push the ACP back behind the line. His phone pings. There's a text message. He reads it and then informs us: 'The police haven't collected any passports from your place, but they did put out an alert in time so Akbar couldn't have left the country. At the very least, he cannot fly from any Indian airport.'

'How else can he leave the country?'

'Well, he can drive into Nepal or maybe even Bangladesh, which is a rather long drive so we can rule that out. Pakistan he cannot enter without a valid visa, so that leaves him with just Nepal, but I doubt it very much.'

'Oh God, when will this end?'

'Don't lose hope, Anush. OK, I'll leave you two and drive to your place to check on the passports.' Aanya gets up and leaves.

'Do you think I drink a lot, Sid? Was it the alcohol or the drugs that made me unconscious? I just want to know.'

'What do you mean by a lot?'

'Excessive?'

'It's all relative, isn't it? What's excessive for an ant is negligible to an elephant.'

'Thanks for that metaphor and thank you for calling me an elephant.'

'I didn't mean that, and you know it. You're gorgeous, and you know that too.'

'Why did Akbar send those photographs of me to you?'

'Like I said I have no idea. I found it rather odd and deleted them immediately. I didn't even speak to Aanya about them until I told you. If he sent them to anyone else, I don't know.'

Thirteen

Mademoiselle Kamala Jha saunters into my room at ten past three, with the same constable in tow. She's in uniform, with a smug smile pasted on her face, which disappears when she sees Sid with me in the room. Perhaps she knew Aryan wouldn't be in at that time and had hoped to get a chance to grill me alone. She says a cursory hello to me, then looks askance at Sid.

'ACP Kamala Jha,' she says in an unruffled, assertive tone. 'I'm investigating the homicide of Mr Rajiv Pant and the attempted homicide of Mrs Anushka Khan here.'

'Sid Dhariwal,' Sid says with aplomb and stretches out his hand. Dhariwal isn't as common a surname as Singh or Khan or Patel. The Dhariwal family name, however, appears in many familiar places. They own and develop more real estate in Delhi–NCR than any other builder in any other part of the world. Aanya and Sid Dhariwal's names appear on flyers, billboards, newspaper advertisements. If you live in Delhi it's impossible to miss it. They have become synonymous with the best houses in the capital. Without stereotyping or offending feminism: he builds the walls, she makes it a home. Every potential luxury homeowner knows DHL: Dhariwal Homes Limited. Customers perceive it as buying a home, not a flat or a house. You cannot miss the Dhariwal name even if you're in Delhi for just a day. That family name practically keeps their marriage going despite the two living separate lives from the beginning – Aanya and Sid are partners in something vastly bigger. Their business is so spread out in the capital that there is a very slim chance the name doesn't reverberate in the ACP's mind. She just needs to figure out if Sid is from the same family. I don't want to tell her he is not just from the family, but heads the empire with his wife.

'I'd like to speak to Anushka alone, if that's OK with you,' she says.

'And I'd like to stay with her while you speak to her, ma'am.' Polite. Soft-spoken.

'Unless, of course, you tell me Anush here is a suspect I am sure it is well within her rights to have a friend with her, especially considering the fact that she's not in the best of mental states at the moment – given what she's been through in the past few days.'

'She's not a suspect, of course.'

'Thank you. I'll stay then.' Sid is as courteous as he is firm.

'Fine by me.'

'As a matter of fact, you should insist she has someone with her every time you come to see her.'

'Should I take that as a warning, Mr Dhariwal?'

'If you must.'

I can see that the atmosphere in the room has suddenly turned tense, and justifiably so.

'How are you, Mrs Khan?' she begins. The friendliness has evaporated from her tone. She addressed me as Anushka last night when she visited me. Now I'm Mrs Khan all over again.

'Nothing's changed since last night when you visited me.' With everything that's happening, I take it upon myself to be a little impulsive, a bit unruly.

'You were here last night?' Sid feigns surprise.

Kamala is a police officer. She knows when to drop the façade, and when not to lie. I bet she's guessed that I've already spoken to Sid, and that we are pretending this has just come up. 'Oh, that… that was just out of courtesy, to check on Mrs Khan.' She looks at me and dares me to challenge her, but I don't. I'm sure she can see on our faces that we've colluded, that we have worked out a strategy. She might've thought I'd give in to her manipulation, but that doesn't mean she's too stupid to reassess the situation now. Sid, I'm certain she has recognised by now, and she knows he's stayed back in the room to make a strong impression. She's smart enough to have worked it all out. 'You can stay if you want to, Mr Dhariwal.'

'Thank you, ACP Jha.'

'We are here to ask if you can think of anything that can lead us to your husband, Mr Khan.' All formal now.

'No she doesn't,' Sid responds before I can and I can see that Kamala isn't pleased.

'I agreed that you can stay here, but that does not mean you answer on Mrs Khan's behalf, Mr Dhariwal.'

'Let me repeat my question: is Mrs Anushka Khan a suspect? Because from what you've just told me, on the records she's not. In which case it shouldn't matter who answers your questions as long as they are answered correctly. Am I right?'

'You are right, but Mrs Khan not being a suspect now does not rule out her becoming a suspect at a later date.' ACP Kamala is quick with her comeback.

'What could she be suspected of? Of concealing the fact that she knows where her husband is holed up? Why would she hide Akbar after he's physically assaulted her? Look at her.'

'Mr Dhariwal, I've been in the police long enough to see all kinds of tricks being played. I'm not saying that Mrs Khan is complicit in her husband's escape after he murdered Mr Rajiv Pant, with whom she was physically involved…'

Thank God I confessed to Aanya and Sid about Rajiv because this bitch had every intention of disclosing that.

'I know Anush and Rajiv had a brief liaison, like you say. Which contradicts your entire hypothesis, doesn't it? If Anushka was involved with Rajiv at any point – emotionally or physically – and that is the motive for his murder, why in the world would she withhold information about his murderer?'

'The answer is quite apparent if you think rationally, Mr Dhariwal. Anushka *had* an affair with Rajiv – like you said, and like she has admitted – but she is still married to Akbar Khan. She is still Akbar's legally wedded wife, so it's not difficult to imagine why.'

'And that's the logic that brought you to her hospital room after hours to try and convince her to entrap Akbar?'

'No.'

'Why then? And please don't try to deny your visit because what you don't know is that we have a video recording of your visit here.' Sid points at the little lens in the corner.

ACP Kamala Jha nods, very slightly. She turns to Constable Bhim Singh and, with a movement of her finger, asks him to leave the room. I guess this interview is over without me uttering a word. Sid pushed her back behind the line, as he said he would.

The constable leaves without questioning his superior. The customary squeak of the door makes the other two look in that direction. Funny how you get used to irritating sounds over time.

'Do you want to ask me something, Mr Dhariwal?' ACP Jha asks.

'I'm not asking anything. I am merely saying that your visit last night to see Anushka *without consent*' – he strongly emphasises the last two words – 'wasn't appropriate. I'm not here to interfere in your investigation or cause any problems, however I cannot let a senior-ranking police officer like yourself harass my friend when she's not in the best of health and is going through the trauma of her husband being accused of murdering someone she cared about.'

I love Sid.

'I take your point, and I apologise.' ACP Kamala, it's apparent, has realised she's blundered. How would she have known there was a camera in the room? That her visit and her conversation – bordering on illegal – had been captured. 'I'm sorry,' she says looking at me.

'It's OK.' Those are my first words since she's come into my room. 'I guess we all are aligned in aiming for the same thing here – all of us want to find Akbar, to know what exactly happened on Saturday night. Why did he drug me, why did he shoot Rajiv?'

'Well, why he shot Rajiv isn't too hard to guess, but yes, there are a million other questions,' Sid responds to my rhetoric.

'I'm glad we all agree on that. If you think judiciously, you might accept why any police officer investigating this case might be compelled to think Anushka has a motive to conceal if she knows where Akbar Khan is,' ACP Kamala says.

'Not when Akbar has done this to her. He drugged her and she was his next target after he had finished with Rajiv. He called Rajiv to their house for God's sake…he had every intention to harm them both. Anushka had enough wits about her to call the police before she passed out, and that's the sole reason she is alive today.'

ACP Kamala Jha nods.

Sid's phone pings.

'Excuse me,' he says and pulls out his phone. He shows the ACP the message before passing the phone over to me. It's from Aanya – Akbar's passport is missing. Found Anush's passport.

Fourteen

'We put an alert out to all the authorities; I am confident Akbar Khan cannot have travelled out of the country,' Kamala defends her department.

'Wrong. He couldn't have flown out of the country. We discussed this before you came in. He can easily drive out of India if he gets to the Nepal border, and you know that,' Sid says.

'Do you know what countries your husband holds valid visas for?' the ACP asks.

'I'm sure he has valid ones for the UK and the US.'

'Well, if we rule out that he took a flight from Delhi, his car should have been captured on some camera, some service station where he stopped to refuel or rest or to relieve himself?'

'It's not as simple to coordinate efforts from every state, Mr Dhariwal. Did he have a lot of cash on him, would you know?' she asks me.

'I don't know. He always has cash on him. I don't know how much he had on this occasion.'

'Because we have already informed the banks. If he uses his credit or debit cards, we'll know. And it's been almost four days, and there's been no activity. Fascinating, isn't it? Amid a crisis like this – where you've killed another human being – your friend, your wife's alleged lover – you have the presence of mind to carry your passport and enough cash before you up and run for your life.'

'Well, we all have to admit, Akbar is certainly a smart guy,' Sid picks up on the ACP's analysis. 'This wasn't a spur-of-the-moment thing, and it cannot be presented like that in any court.' He shoots down the ACP's hyperbolic theory from last night.

I'm fascinated and anxious, all at the same time, to see two people working it all out while I lie prone on the hospital bed without having any say. It's like being a spectator in my own life.

'What do you mean?'

'Akbar knew what he planned to do – agreed?' The ACP and I nod.

'When Akbar heard that Anush was on the phone calling the police, he knew it was time to leave – agreed?'

We nod again.

'He must have known – he has above-average intelligence, as we already know – that the police would arrive at the scene of the murder quickly. In minutes, not hours. He'd have known how close the nearest police station is and, if an emergency call is placed, how soon the police would arrive – agreed?'

Nods again.

'Obviously what he didn't know was that the closest police station would message the next nearest police station that has someone who can head a murder investigation, so there was a delay of five to ten minutes, maybe?'

'What are you getting at?' I ask.

'Hold on a minute, Anush.' I can see the cogs in his brain moving, he's talking as he's thinking through his hypothesis, it is obvious.

'Sorry,' I murmur.

'Anyone in their right mind would know the first thing the police will do if they arrive at the scene of murder and find the alleged accused missing?'

'By the book, we'll put out an alert to the airports to stop a murderer from fleeing the country.'

'And that's what you did.'

'Yes.'

'And still, he thought it was a great idea to carry his passport along with him. Why?'

'You mean, he intended to leave the country for good. Or at the very least, until the investigation is closed.'

'Why?' I interject.

'Exactly, like we discussed earlier. If he crosses the border into Nepal, nothing will stop him from taking a flight to anywhere from Kathmandu. It's quite straightforward. Why would the authorities stop Akbar Khan from taking a flight from Kathmandu to Dubai, London, New York or onwards to somewhere without an extradition policy?'

'You mean he…' I can't stop myself from breaking down yet again.

'Yes, if he can get away, he will, Anush. And I don't think he's planning to return – quite frankly, he doesn't have a choice after what he's done. I bet he knows that if you've survived, you'll know by now that he had drugged you too.'

'But…he had a choice…he shouldn't have—'

'All that is hypothetical now, Anush. It's done. The good news is you are safe – he isn't around to come to the hospital to cause you any harm. He's gone.'

'That's the good news – that my own husband will not come back to kill me? What's the bad news then?'

'You're in this all alone…'

Sid comes close to my bed and bends down to cuddle me.

'How will he manage in a foreign country?'

'You're talking about financial details, Mrs Khan?' ACP Jha is back to her formal self.

'There are ways and means. Did you two keep all your money in joint accounts?'

I look at Sid. 'I don't even know.'

'Anush married Akbar when she was quite young. Akbar handles all the finances. I bet she doesn't know about all his finances and assets. ACP Jha, you already know that Akbar Khan is an erstwhile nawab – he's never worked a day in his life, but he has enough money to buy a small town or a city, trust me. I bet even he doesn't know how much he's worth.'

The ACP looks at me, startled. Really? She wants to ask but doesn't. 'So you think he is capable of leaving a battered wife and just vanishing?' she asks instead.

'What's option B?' Sid asks. 'You think he'll be a martyr and come back to spend the rest of his life in a prison cell?'

I can't believe this is being said in my presence, but what's there to conceal any more?

'We are with you, Anush. You don't have to feel alone, ever. We are your friends.'

As if on cue, I hear the now familiar pipe of the door. Aanya has returned after visiting my house, she has retrieved my passport.

'How did we miss that?' the ACP asks but it's rhetorical.

'My wife.' Sid introduces Aanya to Kamala. 'Is there any way you can communicate with the authorities in Nepal to check if a passenger named Akbar Khan has flown out internationally from Kathmandu?'

'I can check, but internationally they don't care if the threat isn't imminent. If we had moved to stop him in time, yes they would have certainly helped. Asking if he's already gone – not so helpful. I'll put in a request, but I won't hold my breath on it.'

'Thank you.'

'We recovered the murder weapon – the gun – and on analysis, we only have your husband's fingerprints all over it. There's nothing to suggest that Rajiv Pant ever held or touched the gun.' ACP Kamala looks at me sympathetically, or maybe apologetically, considering that last night she was the one proposing that we could position the entire episode as a heated argument between the two men that led to a scuffle and that the gun might have been fired by accident. There was no evidence of that. 'I think I should be leaving now.'

'Can I ask when I will get my mobile back, please? All my contacts are in the device…'

'I'll ask someone to get it to you tomorrow morning. Unfortunately, Akbar's phone will be kept as evidence.'

I nod.

'Thank you, ACP Jha,' Sid says.

'Thank you for being there for your friend. Can I ask for some discretion? I was just trying to be—'

'Don't worry about it at all. I promise I'll destroy the tape.' Sid doesn't even check with me. To be fair, we haven't even seen the alleged recording. We don't even know how much of our conversation last night was captured on the camera. It was dark, and the voices might have been muffled, but Sid handled the whole afternoon brilliantly, I have to admit. Confidence, as they say, is always the ace, king and queen, and Sid has them all in his pocket, and he played his cards dazzlingly.

THURSDAY, 11TH JULY

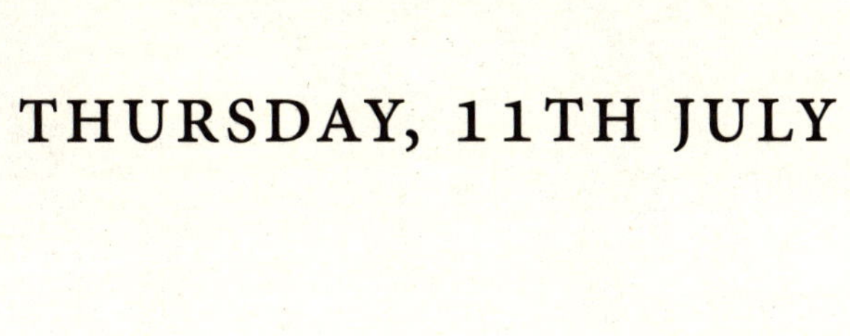

Fifteen

I can't wait to get out of here now. The hospital stench is killing me. And it's not just the smell. I feel trapped, heavy. Aryan has started coming across as a lovesick puppy. He's become a bit cloying at times. Yes, I wanted him to step in when required, yes he's handsome, and yes, I'm more than happy to be his friend. In another world, under different circumstances, perhaps the relationship could have escalated to a physical or even emotional level, but for now, I have no intention of entertaining his lust. He needs to appreciate that I am still someone else's wife – Akbar's status is still *missing*, not dead. Although I haven't told him anything, I am positive he has heard the news about my affair with Rajiv. Either that or he is smart enough to have put together why Akbar shot Rajiv and why I landed in this hospital bed. In all likelihood, he assumes that if I've strayed once I might be willing to two-time yet again. He isn't aware of the dynamics of my relationship with Rajiv – the how and why.

I close my eyes and fight sleep.

***

A while ago, I came to know that Akbar had hired a private investigator to tail my parents and me in Jamnagar before our wedding. Even the sloppiest of Sherlocks could have uncovered the intricacies of our daily lives. They weren't hidden anyway. The only person who chose to ignore my mother's improprieties was my father. At times, I sympathised with him; at other times, I wanted to hold him, shake him up, shout at him for being a cuckold, a shameless one at that. A coward. But despite my best intentions, I never did. I pondered what would happen if I had broached the subject of my mother's not-so-secret hook-ups at dinnertime one day.

Would my father be left with no choice but to speak up, finally? Did he have any fight in him? Or would I just be shaming him? Because my mother – as far as I know – had no shame left whatsoever. Over the years she had seen me watching her take lovers into the bedroom. She knew I could hear the noises outside the bedroom, knew that I was old enough to understand what was going on inside – we lived in a one-and-a-half-room house, it wasn't like Akbar's palatial farmhouse. When her lovers left, she'd come out, not even bothering to tie her sari back on correctly at times. Maybe she didn't think what she was doing was disgraceful, I don't know. I worried that if I confronted my weak father, he might be forced to take action. What if his reaction was to leave us or end his life? Shame is one thing, but being chastened by your own child might be another level of ignominy.

I should have, but I never dared to ask her why she did it. I realised, in time, that by intentionally overlooking my mother's indecencies, I had truly become my father's daughter.

But that was my past, my parents, my family. It must have taken a sleuth some three days to find all that out. In a small town, everyone knows everyone's business. The rumour mill runs 24/7. The sleuth only had to speak to a few neighbours to put a dossier together. The filth didn't need to follow me when I left Jamnagar. It did, nevertheless. You cannot *un-know* something you know. I bet Akbar couldn't either. For a long time, his veiled remarks were benign enough for me to stay within the lines. You have to appreciate that I was this young, unsophisticated, poor, small-town girl married into wealth. For me, it was the cost of fortune, not something to complain about. I was learning. Over time, and after meeting and getting close to other people in Akbar's clique, I started developing an independent personality, blossoming from a nubile young thing into a woman. You pick up things as you grow, from watching others, speaking to them, and discussing their growing pains. I saw women at parties in outfits that could put my mother to shame. And the realisation began to dawn on my still-burgeoning brain that a woman dresses for herself. How low she ties her sari or how much skin she shows is exactly what *she's* comfortable with, and it's not anyone else's business, not even her husband's. And for those who think otherwise, it's your problem. I wear what I wear for myself. It does not mean I am trying to woo you. Yes, I want to look attractive and pleasing to the eye, but it's for me. *Me.* Not you.

Akbar, sadly, did not subscribe to my views.

The personal attacks turned into bullying when I disregarded his opinion and wore a backless dress or one that was 'too short'.

If we were attending a social evening, he was always ready early. He'd have a cigarette – he smoked when I married him, and quit later – and then he would go and sit in the car and wait for me, honking every minute to make me aware that he was waiting. It was only when I came out of the house and sat in the car that he'd take note of my outfit and pass a rude comment and by then, it would be too late to go back and change. He'd torment me all the way to the host's place for wearing what I wore. Then – perhaps he watched me all evening – he would note how many men spent how much time talking to me, who was staring at my legs or cleavage, and so on – and the journey home would become a nightmare. Once we were back home, he'd just discard me like a used tampon and go to sleep in his study.

In the years that followed, it was as if he graduated from a master's in bullying to a PhD. Thrice, he slapped me across the face for being too much of a rebel, and it's all my fault for not walking out on him or exposing his untoward behaviour. He had this innate ability to woo me back in the morning by apologising, bringing me flowers and breakfast in bed, giving the servants time off and making love to me like it was the first time. And promptly, I pushed his temper, his violent personality, behind us. He's my husband and he loves me, I would tell myself. If he feels jealous, it means he's still in love – lies I told myself to continue a life I was so lucky to have been married into.

But it only got worse.

He broke a cardinal rule. Marriages are private affairs. What happens behind closed doors – the good, the bad and the ugly – should remain strictly private. One evening, that changed.

Rajiv was Akbar's only bachelor friend, and Akbar had invited him over for drinks and dinner, and a possible *stay-overnight-if-you-get-drunk* sort of evening.

They were already halfway through their first drinks of the evening when I stepped out to greet him. I could immediately sense that Akbar wasn't happy to see me, from the way his face started turning red. I wore an LBD – a little black dress – which really was little, I won't lie. But again, I had dressed for myself. I was comfortable showing my legs, and if, when I sat, Akbar and his friend wanted to look closely and peek underneath, I was wearing long knickers.

As the evening and drinks progressed, Rajiv complimented me a few times too many for Akbar's liking. That was it.

'My wife will be re-enacting the famous scene from *Basic Instinct* by uncrossing and crossing her legs in a bit,' he started. 'By the way, do you know her mother was a whore?' No mincing words. No editing. Akbar broke all marital and honourable boundaries that evening.

I didn't know what to say. Rajiv didn't know where to look. He gathered, and rightly so, that if he looked at me or my legs one more time, Akbar's fuse might blow. It was almost eleven in the evening, and we had been drinking for over three hours by then. There was no way Rajiv could drive, but he excused himself.

'I think I should leave now.'

'No, you can't. I don't think you can physically drive now, forget the legality,' I said.

'You can't say no to such a sexy offer, can you?' Akbar humiliatingly gestured with his hands towards me moving them from my head to my toes to make a point.

'Guys, I'm sorry if I said—'

'Oh, shut up, Rajiv – don't be a saint. You've spent the entire evening trying to look up her short dress, and I can't blame you. Like mother, like daughter – what do they say…a rotten apple doesn't fall very far, does it?'

I wanted Akbar to drop dead. To hold his tongue, to stop. But he didn't. He couldn't. His vitriol was toxic and relentless. Once he started, he went from my mother to me. Trashed the weakness of my father, called him impotent, and used the choicest swear words in Hindi. He disparaged me, killed the little confidence I had built up since the wedding, and reduced me to the status of a harlot, telling me in no uncertain terms that I was a lower-class whore, undereducated by his standards, unworthy of him and his heritage. He told me, in as many words, that he could afford a harem full of younger and better-looking girls than me, and that he'd do just that.

Rajiv attempted to intervene amidst his lengthy abusive monologue, but Akbar would have none of it. He accused our guest of being a pervert.

I tried to talk him down, but he went berserk if I uttered a word. I went up to him to physically calm him, and he slapped me across my face so hard that I fell down. Rajiv rushed to pick me up, and that gave Akbar more fodder to point out that I wanted the physical proximity of another man. A no-win situation really.

Rajiv left. I have no idea how. Did he drive that night? He shouldn't have. Did he call someone once he was outside to come and drive him home? We don't know because he slammed the door and was gone.

Akbar continued his hectoring long after. He was vicious.

***

I can only blame myself. When I woke up and analysed the situation, my choices were fairly limited. I could continue to be the wife of an erstwhile nawab – I didn't care much about his heritage – but the riches had, of course, changed my life. It's not funny how easily and quickly one gets used to good things in life, and giving them up can be terrifying. I couldn't imagine my life back home in Jamnagar, not being able to afford the luxuries I had become used to by then. I needed all the comforts without the bullying and the slaps and the humiliation.

And when Rajiv called me the next morning, I was in a state of near breakdown from what had happened in his presence the night before. He comforted me, telling me it was a one-time thing, that Akbar had gone over the top, that he had lost control, and that it shouldn't have happened but it did and we should all bury the incident and move on. He asked if I wanted to meet, as a friend, to comfort each other and I took up the offer.

I drove to his place.

One thing turned into another. You know what I mean? What started as a comforting hug between two friends inadvertently turned into unzipping each other's clothes. Did I resist? Did I capitulate easily? At any rate, my words couldn't keep pace with my body's response to his touch. Did I want it? I wouldn't dwell on that. No point. It wasn't planned, but neither of us tried to stop it either. The lovemaking was intense. I can't even describe how good it felt. He was considerate and loving, caring. Somehow, the despicable events from the night before weren't discussed. Surprisingly, what had brought us together wasn't addressed on any occasion ever after that. Perhaps that was the beauty of the relationship. We didn't want the ugliness of the night in question to overtake the allure of this simple oasis we were in together. Before I knew it, I was making excuses to go shopping during the day, to steal a few hours to go to a mall in Gurgaon since Rajiv's apartment was close by. Knowing how keen-eyed and vigilant Akbar was, I didn't take any chances. I always took a shower in Rajiv's apartment, scrubbed myself clean after making love, taking no risk of leaving a scent or a trace of him on me.

Rajiv had a terrific sense of humour, which, if you were meeting him for the first time, you might find a bit over the top. Not as handsome as Akbar, he also lacked the self-confidence Akbar had. While Akbar was cocky, Rajiv was more affable. But where Rajiv really fell short was that he was devoid of any ambition; the drive was missing. He came across as someone who needed to be led and not the other way around. A perfect friend for Akbar if you believe that opposites attract. He didn't have Akbar's sharp cheekbones and long eyelashes, but he had an artistic touch about him. He was a professional painter, and among those in Akbar's circle, he was the only one who was visibly financially struggling. Not struggling like my father, but compared to the others he socialised with, he was. Akbar had been Rajiv's patron for a long time, and that scared him. If Akbar made one negative comment about Rajiv or his work, the doors to art galleries would unquestionably close, he told me. He knew he was walking a thin line.

And while I could understand Rajiv's predicament if we got caught, I didn't even want to imagine mine.

While sex with Akbar was good – what did I really know? I was a virgin when I met him – Rajiv awakened me sexually. Isn't a woman at the peak of her sexual desires around thirty? Rajiv showed me a side of myself I didn't know existed. Sometimes it felt as though he was using me. Then again, we were both using each other and enjoying it. I would have sex with Rajiv in the day, and again with Akbar at night. Sex had become routine and mundane with Akbar, and it might sound cliché, but the excitable afternoons with Rajiv sort of rejuvenated the fire between us, husband and wife. Did I feel guilty? Yes and no. I knew I had to stop. I *should* have before…before it came to this. If I had only pulled my hedonistic head out of the sand and reasoned, I would have certainly chastised myself for now having become my mother's daughter. How was this different? OK, I wasn't taking money or gifts from Rajiv – on the contrary I was, on several occasions, more than reasonably generous to him with Akbar's money – but I was an adulterer nevertheless. Where did I fit on the scale of morality now? Akbar and I hadn't been married long but somehow the sex wasn't as new or ravishing as it had been in the beginning. I wondered if that was simply what happened after a few years of being together. The thought of the next forty to fifty years of boring marital sex agonised me. Of course, that didn't mean I should be getting it elsewhere.

I don't know what daftness we shared that the idea of Akbar coming to know about these assignations never occurred to either of us. Although subliminally it was present in my mind, Rajiv and I never spoke about that damn elephant in the bedroom. We did not once discuss how devastating the repercussions would be if Akbar found out. Even more daft was the way we carried on in the belief that we'd never get caught. Really?

But like all secrets, this one had to come out too.

I distinctly remember that evening – 15th July. Our wedding anniversary. Rajiv and Akbar had made up after Akbar had profusely apologised to his friend more than a few times since that fateful night when Rajiv had left our home unceremoniously. Fortunately, we didn't spend any social evenings with Rajiv alone after that; we only met either at a friend's place or at the club or at a restaurant. Always with another couple around, at least. Neither man spoke about that unpleasant evening – at least not in my presence – and what was there to talk about? If the relationship had to continue, that was the best option.

This was our anniversary get-together, at our place. Over thirty close friends had been invited, and the caterers had been called in. It was one of the cooler July evenings in Delhi, and the little party took place on the front lawns. Despite my strong convictions, I decided to dress conventionally. A pink sari, similar in colour to the one I wore at my wedding reception.

Rajiv was invited too, and I had warned him not to come anywhere close to me. We even debated whether it might be a good idea for him to avoid coming over, but then he would be conspicuous by his absence. A lot of friends would ask questions, some might wonder if there'd been a fallout, which could be detrimental to their relationship going forward. In the end, we decided he should come, maybe stay for a while and then make an excuse to leave. Perfect plan.

A few drinks in, and all that planning went to waste. He wore a white linen shirt and stylish jeans. The attraction was mutual and primal. My nerve endings were tingling. And we made a blunder.

When everyone else was busy with drinks and finger food, or chatting in small groups, we thought it would be safe to wander off outside, to the garden, to steal a kiss. His hands were on the small of my back, I was glued to him, and as we kissed I knew we'd been spotted. Someone – and I would never know who – had surely had a beer too many and had just walked a little way to take a piss in the garden instead of going inside. Disgusting, yes, but I was hardly in a position to admonish anyone. We heard footsteps, we saw a man's shadow move, but we couldn't risk getting close enough to see. Whoever it was must have definitely seen us, and instead of walking in on us or making a scene, had quietly retreated into the party and blended into the crowd.

Thankfully, nothing happened when we rushed back to join the party. The evening was fabulous. Rajiv made an excuse, and despite everyone requesting him to stay a while longer, he left.

Did the person who saw us in an embrace ever tell on us? I don't know. Who was it? I don't know, but I knew Rajiv and I had to be very careful if we were to continue with our affair. Rajiv had looked scared too.

Partly out of guilt, partly due to my family history, I decided we should wind it down a bit before ending our secret affair altogether – we had to economise our trysts, if not end them that very instant.

Sixteen

Aanya and Sid are back to see me this evening. It seems strange that only four of Akbar's and my common friends have cared to visit me in the hospital. Since news of Rajiv and my affair broke out, it strikes me now that by eschewing me all the others have obviously picked a side: Akbar's. I can't say I blame them as they hardly know the truth, and when it comes down to it they're all part of the same Richie Rich club. As for me, I always knew Aanya and Sid were close to me; Monica and Piyush had pleasantly surprised me. But I have resolved that I will not hold anyone's choice against them. When marriages break and couples split – is the wife's breach of marital vows a serious enough transgression for a marriage to break?

Sid gives me an outline of the investigation so far. 'The police still don't know Akbar's whereabouts. Same news on any trace of him using credit or debit cards too. The car hasn't been seen by anyone either—'

'So much for it being conspicuous.'

'The police are hopeful about it being captured by some camera after midnight on Saturday, approximately around the time Akbar must have driven out of Sainik Farms, and they're trying their best to chart the route he might have taken by contacting the owners of cameras on private properties.'

'The trouble is, which route did he take?' Aanya asks.

'Oh, I was candid with them. I told that ACP the other day while with Anush that if Akbar had carried his passport he might have made a run for the Nepal border to take an international flight.'

'You sound confident! Almost as though Akbar called you from a public telephone on the highway,' Aanya joked.

'What else do the police have anyway? They've checked manifests of all domestic and international flights out of Indira Gandhi International Airport and there is no Akbar Khan on any of them.'

'All of it hardly translates to Akbar making a dash for Nepal.'

'Where else could he possibly go, you tell me.'

'Maybe,' I attempt to mediate between husband and wife. 'The police's attempt to speak to the authorities across the border isn't as straightforward as we think. And…I'm hypothesising here, but have the police checked any other airports in the vicinity?'

'What do you mean?'

'Sid's theory that Akbar drove to Nepal to take an international flight is logical, I don't disagree. However, the sheer distance he would need to drive with the nation's police looking for him makes it unrealistic. If he left at midnight, and the police had issued a red alert for him in the next one or two hours at most, there is no way he could have crossed into Nepal by then. However—'

'If he travelled to another airport within a 250- to 300-kilometre radius, he could have been at his destination by the time the search started on the ground,' Sid completes it. 'Jaipur comes to mind...it's under 300 kilometres and is definitely under five hours in Akbar's car if the traffic had been easy.'

'Or, he could've changed his car,' I say.

'Absolutely. I bet they were looking for a black Mercedes with the specific registration plate. If Akbar managed to dump his car and pick another one – or take a taxi – it would have been impossible for the police to track him. I don't expect the police to stop and search every vehicle.'

'He could have, just as easily, taken a bus or a train. How could you check them?' Aanya asks.

'Take a bus or a train to where?'

'To wherever you think he took a taxi to.'

'Is Jaipur an international airport?' I ask.

'Most certainly. There are flights from Jaipur to Dubai for sure – I know because I took a flight from Dubai to Jaipur last year since there were no flights to Delhi due to fog,' Sid confirms. 'I bet this fact has completely escaped our otherwise conscientious ACP. I don't think she's checked the manifests of international departures from Jaipur.'

'That must require brilliant presence of mind, don't you think?' Aanya sounds sceptical. 'I mean, to have *accidentally* shot someone – let's give Akbar the benefit of the doubt like ACP Kamala told you to – then collect your passport, scheme to go to another city because you hear your battered wife calling the police and fear that you'd be apprehended if you went to IGI Airport. And not just that, to also have had enough composure left to dump your car en route and arrange for alternate transport. As much as I admire Akbar for his wits, I find it extremely far-fetched, almost impossible.'

'I was thinking the same—' I have to concur.

'But both of you are either missing a vital point here or being ostriches with your heads buried in the sand – completely overlooking it when it's staring you in the face.'

'And what is that?'

'That it wasn't an *accident*.'

'How can you say that?' I ask, my voice breaking.

'He drugged you, Anush. He called Rajiv home, he left his phone behind so he could not be traced, and if it was *accidental*, as Aanya just said, why did he bolt? I agree with Aanya that it is impossible to be so cool-headed if it were an accident. I'm saying that it wasn't something that happened in the heat of the moment. This was planned and cold-blooded.'

My sobs are high-pitched now.

'I didn't mean that, I'm sorry.'

'It's not your fault, Sid…it's just that when you put it all together with such methodical logic…it implies…that my husband…had been planning to do this for a while now.'

'I was just thinking aloud; none of us knows the truth,' Sid, seeing me in tears, backtracks on his own hypothesis now.

'But you do realise how horrible it sounded when you contemplated that,' Aanya admonishes him. 'There has to be some misunderstanding, Anush. The police are certainly missing some piece, and we are missing something too. There has to be a reason the police still haven't issued an arrest warrant for Akbar. Every piece of news I've read or heard is urging him to establish contact with the nearest police station so that they can talk to him.' She pulls out her iPhone from her bag and unlocks it.

'I don't want to give anyone false hopes here, but I think that's just a ruse. Once he walks into a police station, he will be arrested, no questions about it.' It is apparent that Sid has made up his mind that Akbar is guilty.

'Hmm...' I don't know how to respond. 'As much as I want to believe you, Aanya, I think I will go with Sid's analysis considering the circumstances.'

'I think I should speak with ACP Jha and ask how she feels about our speculation that Akbar might have, *just might have* attempted to get to Jaipur.'

'I just googled it,' Aanya says, looking up from her phone, 'Chandigarh is almost the same distance from Delhi as Jaipur, if not less. Why do you think Akbar will go to Jaipur and not to Chandigarh, Mr Holmes?'

For once, Sid doesn't have an answer right away. Then: 'OK, I'll ask the ACP to look at manifests for Jaipur and Chandigarh. Basically, any airport within three hundred kilometres or a four to five hour drive from Sainik Farms.'

'Should we speak with her together?' I question between sobs. 'If we are doing her investigation for her, she should also be willing to give us an update.'

'You make a valid point, Anush.'

***

'How are you finding our hospitality?' Aryan drops by on his evening round to check on me. I realise he hasn't visited all day.

'I'm feeling a lot better, although...as my sanity returns, a different kind of trepidation has taken over my mind as you can imagine.'

'I completely understand, Anushka, but you have to be patient. And brave, if I may say so. The senior doctor tells me your stitches are healing well, so unless – God forbid, and fingers crossed – there's any complication that arises tomorrow, I think you will be discharged from the hospital on Saturday morning.'

'Thank you. Thank you for everything, Aryan.'

'Oh, there's no need to thank me or anyone. We've just been doing our jobs.'

'No really, thank you. You sat here all evening until midnight the day I woke up, and I blabbered into the night when you could have gone home and caught a good film on Netflix. You need not have listened to my sordid life story. Then, you took time out of your busy schedule to chaperone me when the police came to see me the first time around; that was definitely above and beyond your duty as a doctor.'

He smiles, a little embarrassed as I appreciate his efforts.

'And I'm really sorry if I talked too much the other night, and revealed some ugly bits of my life from the past, which I've never told—'

'You can trust me on that, I promise I won't ever mention our candid conversation to anyone.'

'Thank you, Aryan.'

'You're welcome. I hope and pray Akbar comes back, and your nightmare is over soon.'

'I will be so happy to introduce you to him.' I can see the reservation in his demeanour as I say this. It's been all over the news – Akbar is being accused of murder in the first degree. Even if he returns, life will never be the same. He must think I'm an idiot to believe that will ever happen.

'Of course.' He is polite. Honestly, I wasn't lying when I mentioned earlier that at another time, under different circumstances, we could have been more than friends. However, I am miles away from myself at this moment and in no mental disposition to think about tomorrow, let alone any further.

FRIDAY, 12TH JULY

Seventeen

'We've been meaning to come for a while, but Mira [pronounced *My-ra* to disassociate from the sixteenth-century devotee of Lord Krishna] was having problems at school, and the head teacher wanted to see both of us urgently,' Monica and Piyush Kumar have come to see me this morning, at around eleven. Mira is their daughter, and in all sincerity, at this point in my life, I find it challenging to pretend to have sympathy to spare for a fourteen-year-old girl having a problem in her chemistry class at school. *Really?* I want to ask. Then again, my problem isn't theirs, just as theirs isn't mine. They are under no obligation to visit me in the hospital. Oh, I'm being mean. They are some of the friends who've come to see me.

'I'm so sorry to hear about Mira.'

'It's OK, we took care of everything, but it was…' The mother continues to elaborate on the exact nature of Mira's issue at school, long after my mind has wandered off to a concatenated matter.

The mention of Mira is a harsh reminder that I have no children. Nawab Akbar Khan decided for me on our wedding night that we would only have babies once I was thirty. *'I want you to look just the way you are until then,'* he had firmly told me and that was it. I was so awestruck at being married to him that I never questioned or argued with his flawed rationale at the time, and later, whenever I tried to bring up the topic he told me – '*We decided that at the time of our wedding, so that's non-negotiable.*' I wonder now, if we had had a child, perhaps Akbar would have been less jealous. And I wouldn't have had the time to be involved with Rajiv. But it's all what-ifs now. It's Friday, and it's my last full day at the hospital. Tomorrow I'll be released. Tomorrow, I'm going home. But… where is home now?

'I will be released from the hospital tomorrow,' I say aloud.

'Where will you go?'

'I wish I could go home, of course,' I say softly and wait to hear why Piyush asked me.

'I don't think the police are out of your property just yet. I doubt if those buggers will allow you to live there while they are still investigating. You should stay with us for a while – anyway, I don't think you should be on your own—'

'Why? Do you think Akbar will return to...' I find it difficult to voice the words.

'No,' Piyush, thankfully, understands. 'I don't think the idiot will return to harm you in any way, that's not what I was suggesting. Whatever happened, I believe, happened in the heat of the moment – no matter what the police or the media are saying – it certainly cannot have gone down like they are portraying. Akbar is an asshole, I'll admit, but he is no psychopath. Yes, he must've called Rajiv that evening, but a lot of us call each other over in the evenings just to catch up. That part of the story amounts to fucking nothing. I guess until Akbar returns, we'll never know why he called Rajiv that evening, but taking that piece of info from call logs and presuming he had called Rajiv home to shoot him point-blank is preposterous. Un-fucking-believable, honestly. Too much of a bloody leap.'

The police don't exactly buy that logic, and I think no court will conclude that a phone call from Akbar to Rajiv and the latter turning up at our residence after an hour is anything more than circumstantial.

'I find it difficult to swallow,' Monica says before I do. 'But...it just might have been that Akbar had phoned Rajiv to warn him in some way. Perhaps Rajiv took it upon himself to turn up – I'm making this up as I speak, so bear with me please – to explain himself or to blame Anush or apologise, and it was then that they argued. Testosterone levels, unquestionably, peaked, and whatever happened, happened. What do you think Anush?'

'It also sounds plausible to me.'

'I've known your asshole of a husband for over a decade, he's never been known to be violent—' Piyush stops. My forehead is still bandaged, albeit much more lightly now, and perhaps the stitches underneath the dressing stop his spiel about his friend's non-violent disposition. 'I'm really sorry, Anush.'

Tears fill my eyes.

'How can you even say something like that?' Monica is looking at Piyush.

'I said I'm sorry. It's a stark reminder of what we all know: however close we are to someone, how much do we truly know them? I had no idea whatsoever that you were going through this kind of domestic abuse while all of us believed you were an ideal couple. I'd have knocked some hard sense into his brain with my fist, trust me, if I had known. No one deserves this.'

I nod; more tears well up. Shame takes over. But I remember reading somewhere: *if you have become them to beat them, why bother?*

'Oh, you don't have to worry about it any more, babe. I'm with you, we're with you. You will come home and stay with us for as long as you want, not just until you get your house back.' Monica comes to my bed and holds my hand.

'Of course, you should stay with us until they find Akbar and he gets a chance to explain himself.'

'I don't care how long the police are in the house. But I'm not going to go and live there until Akbar returns...' I break down now.

'Why not?'

'What will the staff think of me? Aanya told me that the media were referring to my affair with Rajiv as the motive for his murder on Saturday night. They must have realised that their nawab is implicated in a crime instigated by my affair...' I break down completely. 'They'll look at me disdainfully.'

'And what did they think of their nawab when he hit you, babe? You're being too harsh on yourself. Women treated badly tend to look for love and respect elsewhere, I bet some wise guy must've put a statistical correlation together.'

I don't say anything.

***

'The three internal stitches will dissolve, and the two external ones require maybe another two to three days before I can remove them.' Dr Raaj Mehra is talking about sutures after having taken off the bandage from my forehead completely. He thinks some airing of the wound will accelerate the healing. I want to ask, if that was the case why did he put the bandage on in the first place? But it's not for me to question.

Nurse Cynthia is standing beside him and graces me with a big smile as though the doctor has just told me I had the winning lottery numbers.

'Does that mean I have to stay here longer?'

'Not at all. You will be discharged tomorrow morning. We'll probably put a thicker adhesive plaster on it, and give you some spare ones to change daily and when they get wet. You need to be extremely careful, and not let the area get wet or accidentally scratch it. Just routine precautions. You can come in to see one of us any time after next Tuesday. If you have mild pain, I suggest you take paracetamol, there should be no need to take anything stronger. Are you on any medication now?' he asks, but he's checking the folder too, to confirm.

'No.'

'No alcohol for a few weeks, please. And avoid taking any drug – prescription or over-the-counter – except paracetamol, without seeking medical advice, for a month at the very least. And if you feel nauseous or giddy or dizzy or if you feel so weak that you might fall, please, please sit down and ask someone to call the hospital, Mrs Khan. Please adhere to my advice and you will be fine in no time.'

'Thank you, Dr Mehra.'

'Is there anything else you need to know?'

'Is Dr Aryan coming to see me in the evening?' *Why did I have to ask that?* He told me he would come.

Dr Mehra looks at Cynthia.

'Yes, he is on duty this afternoon,' she responds with a big smile again. I want to ask her what happened to her plan of bringing her husband to talk to me, but I don't. The constant smile on her face tells me that all is fine in their household. If not, it is up to her to decide. I already have enough to deal with.

Eighteen

'You're *not* staying with Monica, you're coming with *us*. That's the end of it.' It's good to have just a few close friends who love you so much they fight over you. The others are good only for Instagram. Aanya and Sid have come to see me again this afternoon, and she's upset that I did not decline when Monica and Piyush offered to take me to their home. 'How can she take you home without asking me?'

'In the same way that, at this very moment, you're asking Anush to come with you – I doubt you've consulted Monica. Did you, my dear?' Sid winks at me, smiles.

'Don't you get me started, Sid. Anush is coming with us, I'll be here to pick you up in the morning. Better still, I'm not leaving here until they discharge you tomorrow.'

I smile. 'OK, why don't you speak with Monica and let me know where I'm going?'

'Good plan.'

'OK, if you two are through sorting it out, we have some serious matters to discuss. ACP Jha will be here any—'

The door squeaks.

'Think of the angel, and the angel appears,' Sid says sardonically, as he turns around to see the ACP walk in without her constable.

'Good afternoon, all.' She smiles at Sid's twist on the popular idiom but doesn't comment. She's in mufti again. Does she have another outlandish proposal for me? Thank God Sid is here. Then it hits me. She's likely only here because Sid had asked someone up the command chain to exert some influence on her. Why else would the ACP be interested in discussing an ongoing homicide investigation with someone she had suspected of complicity in the accused's escape?

'How are you today, Mrs Khan?'

'I'm good, thank you, ACP Jha.'

'I take it that you haven't heard from Mr Khan at all?' she asks me, then looks at the other two people in the room.

We all wag our heads in unison. No.

'Do you have any news about him?'

'None at all. It's like he's vanished. And I've checked the manifests of all flights from Jaipur and Chandigarh – thanks for the heads-up on that. It was a slip-up on my part, I should have thought of it, but no harm done since he hasn't flown out from either of the airports—'

'But he could very well have taken a domestic flight under an assumed identity?' Sid asks.

'Certainly, and he could have caught the Rajdhani Express to Kolkata too, and there's no easy way to find him if he's switched identities and changed his appearance. But he's not a career criminal, he's bound to make a mistake and inadvertently leave a clue.'

'So far he's been quite successful at not making any mistake,' Sid remarks.

'But that doesn't mean he won't make one. He will need to withdraw money, rent a hotel room, buy or hire a vehicle...there are so many things that you can't do these days if you leave your real life completely unless he's managed to get a false ID.'

Sid looks at me because I exhale in frustration.

'There is something else I'm here to discuss with you, Mrs Khan. It is rather delicate and I must advise you that it would be ideal if it were just you and me in this conversation. But since you're not a suspect, I know I cannot enforce that.'

'There's nothing they don't know, especially after the media circus,' I almost snap. 'Who released all the details of my personal life to the press, do you know?'

'I'm afraid I have no idea. I'm sorry you have to go through all this at a time like this, Mrs Khan, but if it were me, I wouldn't give it too much thought. Tomorrow the busybodies will get a juicier story and you will be relegated to the back pages before you know it. It happens all the time, believe me.'

'If you say so. What is it you were about to tell me?'

The ACP looks around. The other two nod.

'Just remind me what your husband does, please…I mean what's his profession or business, his source of income, if any, besides his inheritance?'

'I thought you'd already established that by looking through his financial records.'

'I'd like to hear your side of the story, please.'

'Akbar is royalty, as you know. He was born with the proverbial silver spoon. He owns a small palace in his erstwhile principality, Jaanandi, which is near Pataudi in Haryana, and the small but well-preserved family fort is now a boutique resort with a two-room suite exclusively maintained for our personal use. The company that operates and looks after the property pays him a handsome amount quarterly, and realistically speaking, it's a lot more than we can spend. He also has an investment company, with an office on Barakhamba Road in Connaught Place. He goes there two or three times a week, sometimes more, but a staff of ten employees and management is in place and so, Akbar doesn't need to hand-hold them on a day-to-day basis.'

'Anything else?' Kamala asks.

'Not that I'm aware of. Why?'

'I'll answer your questions in a minute, but please let me finish first if that's OK.'

I nod.

'What about bank accounts? Do you know anything about his bank accounts, the money coming in and going out?'

'As far as I am aware, I'm a joint account holder in both his personal and business accounts on an either-or-survivor basis, so yes, I have access to his accounts. Obviously, I don't see every account statement that drops through the mailbox or keep tabs on how much he withdraws or when—'

'I was more keen to know if you are aware of the money coming in, Mrs Khan.'

'What do you mean?' Sid asks.

'Mr Dhariwal, can I request that you not intervene in my conversation with Mrs Khan, please?' So ACP Kamala might have come here to talk to me in the hospital and agreed to meet me with Sid and Aanya present, but she wasn't going to bend over backwards and let them derail her from her line of questioning.

'I'm sorry.'

'Thanks. I'm not being rude, but if everyone starts asking questions, I won't get the answers I've been looking for, and it makes the case all the more complicated.'

Sid nods.

'No, like I said, while I'm a joint account holder in the two accounts he has at two different banks…' I tell her the names of the banks. 'I've never bothered to check the bank balances simply because my ATM card or credit card never got declined, so there was no reason to.'

'What if I told you that your husband's income far exceeds the money he earns from the two sources of income you just mentioned?'

'How is that possible?'

'What if I further told you that there are two bank accounts, apart from the two joint accounts you hold, which are exclusively in the name of your husband?'

I look at Sid, then Aanya. 'What are you saying, ACP Jha?'

'By the way, these two other accounts we've uncovered aren't quite in his real name. One is held by Akbr Khan, with a slightly different spelling, and the other is listed as belonging to Akbar K Jaanandi, the name of his principality.'

My hands come up to cover my open mouth. 'No!'

'And these are the only two we've discovered so far.'

'How much money do these accounts have?'

'Crores. Funnily enough, a lot comes in sporadically, but withdrawals are almost negligible.'

'When were these set up?' I'm curious now.

'A couple of years after your wedding and hence, I thought you might have some idea about them or the money.'

'This is the first I've heard of them. What do you think is his source of income other than the two I told you about?'

'Hawala. We think your husband is involved in money laundering on quite a large scale, given the amounts flowing in. We followed the money and this was the obvious conclusion. Hawala runs on word of mouth and verbal assurances and informal record-keeping so it will be almost impossible to prove, but we've identified a few brokers who have confirmed that Akbar Khan is knee-deep in this.'

'You are shitting me.'

'Mr Dhariwal, please...'

Nineteen

Even I want to swear loudly. What kind of illicit mess has my husband been involved in? An even bigger question – how much of an unwitting involvement do I have in his business? I can feel dread taking over.

'Mrs Khan...?' I hear ACP Jha say, in case I've missed what she said.

'Sorry, it is too much for me to swallow...what were you asking?'

'Did you know about any of this?'

'Nothing whatsoever. I always believed we didn't need any more money than we already had. We are barely able to spend what we earn, plus there are vast reserves so I can't see the point of Akbar trying to make more. Why?' *Only to be generous to people like Rajiv?*

'I wish one of us was enlightened enough to answer that one, Mrs Khan. His connections to various ill-reputed people with criminal backgrounds will be scrutinised, so be aware that the media will pick up on that too, and I can only apologise for that in advance.'

'Can't you put an embargo on the media?'

'*I* can't.' She looks at Sid who, she knows, has been pulling strings. He blinks.

'I'll see what I can do, Anush, but it is going to be difficult.'

Is he involved in the hawala business too? The thought races through my mind. But before I can dwell on that, the ACP starts again.

'As part of the investigation, we also visited Mr Rajiv Pant's apartment in Gurgaon. The search teams discovered evidence that corresponds to three significant conclusions. One, of course, is that you had an affair with him. Contrary to your statement, it wasn't a short-lived one. It was a much longer relationship and a more intense one than you wanted us to believe.' She looks at me, challenging me to refute her. 'You're sure you want your friends here while I talk about this?' she asks.

I nod. What's there to conceal from these two now? I've already acknowledged that we were in a physical relationship. Whether Rajiv and I fornicated ten times or a hundred is irrelevant. I never said it was a one-time thing. I look back at her defiantly. 'Yes.'

'The team found one section of his wardrobe full of your clothes and lingerie, which is a sign that you spent much time with him at this apartment.' She stares at me.

'It wasn't so much about spending time with him at his apartment. It was more that I needed to change before I returned so I did not carry his smell or DNA or anything back home.'

'Fair enough.'

I turn towards Aanya, close my eyes and mouth an inaudible *sorry.*

'Secondly – and this might shock you or upset you – but did you know that Mr Rajiv Pant had a hidden camera in his bedroom to capture your trysts?'

'WHAT?'

'Oh yes, there are enough provocative, naked and in flagrante photographs of you to fill a pornographic magazine, Mrs Khan.'

A waterfall blurs my vision. I realise these are more tears of shame than of fear. I shake my head. Aanya is holding my hand again, comforting me. She communicates, without words, that she's with me.

'ACP Jha – sorry to speak out of turn – but how can you ensure that none of those photographs are leaked? To members of your team, to the press, to the public?' Aanya's voice is firm.

'You can trust me with that. I cannot help that some of the team members have seen the photos, but they are now locked and kept safer than the Crown Jewels.'

'Thank you.'

'I understand the need for privacy, and as I mentioned, these are not your normal variety…'

She just couldn't stop herself from adding that. But...but...it's not her. I am the one who was a fool. A stupid, filthy whore. What was I thinking? *'You are amazing on your knees, Anush.' 'You love the taste, don't you? Keep going.' 'How about you lie on your stomach and I take you from behind?' 'You're such a good bitch, let's play doggie.' 'Have you ever had someone up the Hershey's way?'*

All sordid remnants of a bad dream.

I just keep my mouth shut because I don't want to make something bad infinitely worse by cursing out loud at Rajiv. Saying I wish him dead is pointless. He already is. Moreover, such an exclamation might not go down well with the police.

'So here's the thing that's been bothering me, Mrs Khan.' ACP Jha has an uncanny ability to bring me back to the present, as always.

'What is it?' I ask in a voice as meek as a mouse's.

'Is it possible that Rajiv Pant was blackmailing your husband using your photographs?'

I break down completely.

'ACP Jha, you'll have to give Anush a break—'

'I, too, was thinking this, Mr Dhariwal. But as you can understand, these questions need to be asked to get to the truth.'

'Of course. Why don't we let Anush come home with us tomorrow, and we can all meet at our residence in the evening?'

'Sounds good. And in the meantime, if any of you receive any call or message from Akbar Khan or come up with any further ideas about where he went, I'll appreciate you giving me a call immediately.'

'Most definitely.'

'OK, I'll leave you all now,' the ACP says.

'Just one thing – you mentioned that your team found evidence of three significant things from the search at Rajiv's place: what was the third one?' Sid asks.

Thank God he's been paying attention; my brain is completely wrecked by disbelief, discovering all these new things about both my husband and my lover. I silently implore and hope there's nothing more.

I think I've heard the absolute worst but apparently not.

ACP Jha has another, even bigger bomb to drop before she leaves. 'Oh, I'm glad you asked me. Rajiv Pant was no artist. I mean he could paint, but from what I've gathered from talking to art experts and aficionados, no art gallery of repute would ever buy what he produced. Rajiv Pant was one of Akbar Khan's most trusted hawala pigeons. Art is a fitting front to launder money, Mr Dhariwal. You see, every painting is unique and you cannot compare one artist's work to another in any manner. Consequently, no one can ever ascertain how much an artist has sold a particular piece of artwork for.'

All the air in my lungs comes out with a whoosh! Fuck me, I want to scream.

'Have a good day, all of you.'

My best friend on the wall tells me it's 6.08 p.m.

Twenty

Aanya, Sid and I look at the door as it closes when ACP Kamala Jha walks out. We are all agape, as though any minute she might walk back in and update us on another deplorable discovery.

'What is a hawala pigeon?' Aanya asks.

'It's another word for a courier, someone who carries the money,' Sid explains. 'And it makes sense if you think about it with a cool head. You will only hand over cash worth crores without a receipt to someone you can trust. And Akbar trusts—'

'Trusted,' Aanya corrects. 'At some point, it is evident that the two must've fallen out over something for Akbar to take the extreme step, don't you think?'

'I can't believe it, any of it,' I say.

'Don't take me wrong, Anush, but in a warped, tangential manner, it should take a wee bit of weight off your conscience. It should relieve you of any guilt that Rajiv died because of you. It is entirely possible – and I am positive – that there was another bone of contention between him and Akbar.'

I'm still unnerved, but I make an effort to smile.

***

'Looking forward to leaving us tomorrow then?' I was so exhausted after the long session with the police that I fell asleep after Aanya and Sid left. Aanya promised me that she'd speak to Monica, leaving no ambiguity about the fact that she would be picking me up in the morning. I was not aware when Aryan came into my room, but it seems like he's been here for a while since he has taken readings from all the instruments already. He stands next to my bed now, politely saying goodbye.

'Unfortunately, yes.' I smile.

'Being a doctor, we get that a lot. A lot of people can't wait to get as far away from us as possible and never want to see us again. Occupational hazard, I guess.' He smiles back.

'Could you do me one last favour, Aryan?'

He nods.

'Can I see my face in a mirror, please?' I haven't once done that since regaining consciousness after my ordeal. The hospital authorities have deliberately removed the mirror from the bathroom. I wanted to ask Aanya earlier in the day, but ACP Kamala's visit has been unsettling, to say the least.

'Are you sure?'

'Yes. Please.'

He goes out and returns with a small hand-held mirror, which I'm positive he's borrowed from a nurse's handbag.

I look ghastly. Pale. Worn out, broken, desolate. They've shaved a portion of the hair that I had paid over-the-top money to style – so that it falls over my forehead; they've chopped it off for precisely the same reason: to prevent it from infringing on the sutures. The gash is deep – five stitches, isn't that what the doctor said? – and the wound still appears a little raw to me. Dark circles have formed under my eyes that appear to have sunk back into my skull. Long story short, I look terrible. Without uttering a word I stretch my hand to give the mirror back to him. There's nothing I can do about how I look at the moment. Why cause myself agony by staring at my face?

'Thank you.'

'Not a bother at all.' He takes it. 'I guess it's time to say bye. You'll be gone before I start my shift tomorrow afternoon. Do you need anything from me?'

'No. Thank you once again, Aryan.'

'All the best, and please adhere to all the do's and don'ts as advised.' He points towards a small file that I'm supposed to be carrying back with me. 'If you book an afternoon appointment to remove your stitches, I'll be glad to do it personally.'

'Thank you.'

SATURDAY, 13TH JULY

Twenty-One

'You look so weak after eating the drab hospital chow, we'll cook something as soon as we get home,' Aanya says. I have no clue – and neither do I want to know – how Aanya managed to convince Monica that I am going back with Sid and her to their place. For my own part, if I had a choice I would have decided to go with Aanya anyhow. There's something about them that puts me more at ease than I am with the Kumars.

'Some seafood pasta, please.'

'Not too many carbs in pasta? And seafood isn't good for Anush at the moment.'

'But Anush needs carbs,' Sid says, looking at me in the rear-view mirror as he drives us home to New Friends Colony. There's no more conversation until we reach home. Their two-storey white house is built in the art deco style with powder-coated steel and black Crittall windows. There is a medium-sized Mughal garden that houses a fountain as one enters the drive. It's a huge property especially considering where it's located; in truth, it's a fraction of our farmhouse by size, but this is New Friends Colony after all, one of the poshest residential areas in Delhi. Contemporary art adorns the walls unlike ours where everything is from the days of old. Well, they live in the city, and we live on a farm.

Lunch is penne with garlic and cheese and chillies. It tastes amazing. I go easy on it to avoid my stomach going bad. The last thing I want is to end up in a hospital bed with an upset stomach. Of course, the doctor hasn't prescribed a diet plan but I need to be careful. It's early days still.

'Did you have any inkling that Akbar was into money laundering?'

I look at Sid as though he's asking me if I've ever attempted to jump off the Eiffel Tower. I suppose my expression is enough to indicate how ludicrous it is to think I knew about any of it.

'I didn't mean—'

'I know your heart is in the right place, Sid. You don't need to explain. It isn't a secret to you two that I come from a very modest background, but I was truthful when I told the ACP that the money we legitimately earn from the fort leased to the hotel group doesn't get spent. It gets added to the money that's already sitting in the bank. I don't need more, we can't possibly spend it all, it's just the two of us for now. There's enough to go around even if we had two children in the next two years. Enough to pay for their upbringing, schooling, higher education abroad, whatever. I'm surprised – no, I'm *shocked* Akbar was running the risk…for what?'

'It's never the need, it's the greed isn't it?'

'Believe me, there was enough to satisfy greed too, in Akbar's case.'

'Very reckless, I must say. And to have one of your school buddies involved in an illegitimate business…'

'And I went and slept with him. Out of all the men in this world, the only man I could find was Rajiv Pant.' I put my fork down. I have had a sudden thought. 'Did you know about this, Sid?' I ask.

'Me? No. What makes you think I knew?'

'Are you sure?' Aanya picks up the baton. 'If I find out you're involved in anything illegal, I won't be as patient as Anush. I'll call the police.'

'Calm down, Aanya. I said I'm not doing anything illegal. Rajiv worked for – or with – Akbar because he had nothing better to do. I'm sorry if that sounds mean, but we all knew he was a subpar painter. Come to think of it, how else could he sustain the lifestyle he was living? If Akbar is indeed into hawala, what better partner could he have picked? Anyone else would have asked a hundred questions, maybe even smacked Akbar on the head, and told him to be sensible, trust me.'

Sid has a point. I knew Akbar helped Rajiv. Now I know why. It was a two-way street. Even I helped Rajiv. In more ways than fiscal, I think. 'My photographs…' My throat constricts. 'Did Rajiv ever send you any?'

'Oh no, not at all. I told you I only ever received a few from Akbar once, and that's that.'

'We shouldn't talk about the dead in that manner, but he was a real bastard to be snapping photographs of private moments with you. I wonder what his intentions were…what time did ACP Jha say she's coming over?' Aanya asks.

'Sometime in the evening after five.'

'I guess you can take a little nap, Anush.'

'I think so too.'

***

'According to the neighbours, Rajiv Pant hadn't been at his apartment since last Friday afternoon,' ACP Kamala Jha arrives in uniform with Constable Bhim Singh in tow at five on the dot. She scans the house by giving it a once-over, settles on the sofa and attempts small talk with us. My brain, however, is racing with questions. I want her to come to the point.

'Why is the focus of your investigation on Rajiv and not Akbar who, when you find him, should be able to explain all of this?' Sid is quick.

'Because we cannot find Akbar, and we are kind of, you know, deconstructing his murder.'

'*Deconstructing his murder?* What does that even mean?'

'Well, the police typically attempt to put together the past couple of days or hours of a victim's movements, then match them to those of the accused, if possible. Or even with others that the victim or accused knew well. There is always a possibility of an overlap: the victim might have been with someone, revealed his state of mind, or may have spoken about certain things that may lead us to a clue or a conclusion. We do the same with the accused. It's vitally important to put these timelines together. Does it make sense?'

It does and it doesn't, but the three of us nod like schoolchildren.

'You think that tracing the last few days of the victim might give you some clues?'

'Oh, the dead do tell tales, believe me, Mr Dhariwal.' ACP Kamala lets out a smile that can only be described as conspiratorial.

'Going back to your point, can I ask how the neighbours know Rajiv hasn't been home since Friday afternoon?'

'A neighbour had gone to invite him to the building society meeting on Friday evening around four. When he did not find Rajiv at the apartment, he left a note on the door handle, which was still there when the police got there on Sunday morning after his death.'

'Perhaps Rajiv came home, read the note, but didn't bother to take it off the door handle?'

The ACP looks at Sid, but does not have to ask: *really?*

'What else did the neighbours tell you?' I ask.

'A few of the neighbours confirm having seen you visiting him on several occasions. Mostly in the afternoons.' Her words are chosen carefully and spoken in a neutral manner. She even beams at me. The *I-know-it-all* beam. Afternoons were the best time to visit Rajiv's apartment, of course. On the days Akbar went to the office at Barakhamba Road, it was the best time for me to slip away under the guise of shopping or running errands. Two to three hours of revelry, a shower, a change and I used to be back home in time before Akbar returned. What I wasn't aware of at the time was that I was being photographed without consent.

'The neighbours thought that you two were dating, they obviously didn't know you were married to someone else,' Kamala continues. 'It's only when the media plastered your photograph with the story that they recognised you.' If she intends to shame me, she's successful. I bet my face is reddening, I can feel the blood rising up my neck.

'We all make mistakes. Anyway you're the aggrieved one here considering what Rajiv did,' Sid says.

'May I know where you were on Friday evening, Mrs Khan?'

'I was at home.'

'Were you home the entire time?'

'Yes.' From the corner of my eye, I see the constable noting down every bit of our conversation in his notebook.

'What did you do the whole time?'

'I made myself a sandwich and browsed Netflix.'

'Do you remember what you were watching?'

'No. As I said, I was just browsing programmes and there was nothing of interest. But what has that got to do with what happened on Saturday evening?' I know I sound exasperated, but this ACP is truly getting on my nerves now.

'And where do you think your husband was on Friday evening, Mrs Khan?' She notices the irritation in my voice, and although she's visibly annoyed at my questions, she makes a tremendous effort to hide her frustration. She could be a nominee for the Filmfare award this year. *The award for best female actor in a supporting role goes to Ms Kamala Jha.*

'He came home late on Friday evening.'

'Do you know where he'd gone?'

'No. He told me he'd be staying late at the office on Friday as he had some guests visiting from abroad and then he'd take them out for drinks and dinner.'

'Did you ask who was in town? Anyone specific we can check with?'

'No.'

'Do you know which restaurant he took the guests to on that Friday evening?'

'No. I generally never asked about anything regarding his business meetings,' I say curtly.

'I'm sure if he paid the bill on his credit card, we shall find out in time where he went and with how many people. By the way, we checked with the office staff at Barakhamba Road, Mrs Khan, and it might come as a surprise to you, but no business associates were visiting your husband from abroad on that particular Friday. According to them, Akbar Khan left the office shortly after 4.30 p.m.'

'What?'

'And that is of significance because…?' Sid asks.

'To establish if Rajiv and Akbar were together on the previous evening since both of them weren't where they should have been. Maybe Akbar told Mrs Khan he was out for a business meeting, but met Rajiv. If that's the case, where did Rajiv go after Akbar went home? Ah, that reminds me, what time would you say your husband returned home, Mrs Khan?' she asks me. She's not being straightforward, she's slipping in questions between snippets of information she's letting out, making the query seem like an afterthought. I need to be careful with this woman. Nothing she asks will be inconsequential.

'It was definitely late. After I had gone to bed.'

'You have no idea what time it might've been?'

'None at all.'

'Do you remember what time you went to bed?'

'Around midnight.'

'And you're certain he wasn't home by then?'

'I am positive. I'd have known if he came home before then.' I raise my eyebrows to emphasise.

'Was anyone else at home with you that evening?'

Too many questions. 'No. The staff usually leave at six in the evening unless we have guests over, I already told you.'

'That being the case, would I be correct in assuming that Akbar returned home sometime after midnight, using his own set of keys?'

'You will be correct, yes.'

'And you didn't hear any sounds? The car engine, the wheels on the driveway, the door opening, shutting…nothing?'

'No.'

'Did someone…anyone visit your home on Friday evening between six in the evening – when you were all by yourself after the staff left – until midnight when you went to sleep?'

'No.'

'No deliveries either?'

'No.'

'And Akbar, of course, returned home alone.'

'Yes.'

'How would you know that? You were asleep, weren't you?'

'I was asleep, but I would have known if there had been a guest at home when I woke up the following Saturday morning.'

'How would you know that if the guest didn't stay overnight? If they just came in for a nightcap and left after a drink or two? How would you know?'

'I'm pretty sure Akbar would have mentioned it to me if he had brought a friend or a work colleague home for a drink the night before. But I don't know why you're asking me all this.'

'Pardon me for pointing out the obvious, Mrs Khan, but I don't get the impression that your husband told you everything. He seemed to have a habit of deliberately omitting a minor detail or two now and again, which, rather surprisingly, I must add, you never spotted.'

I swallow my pride. There's so much I know about Akbar now that I didn't know until a day ago. All the same, he didn't know everything about my activities either. Did that make us even?

'I'm sorry I have to ask all these annoying questions, Mrs Khan. But it's my job. If we don't probe diligently, we are prone to missing those minor details which can make or break a case.'

I nod.

'Anything you want to ask me?'

'When can I go home?'

'What's the rush?' Aanya asks me.

'Your house is unfortunately still cordoned off, and I can only apologise for the inconvenience. You will have to wait a week or so more. We'll let you know as soon as we vacate the premises.'

'Thanks.'

Twenty-Two

'Mrs Khan, you and Mr Khan got married in…?' ACP Kamala shows no signs of leaving. On the contrary, Aanya asked her if she needed a drink and she requested coffee for the constable and herself. She appears to be here for the long haul. Two hours and counting. At this rate, she might be staying back for dinner with us.

'We got married in two thousand and eleven.'

'And how would you describe your marriage?'

I find the question intrusive, but I respond, 'Like all marriages,' as calmly as possible.

She gives me that quick, all-knowing smile again, which I am starting to loathe. And as though her foxy smile isn't enough she says, 'Mrs Khan, wives don't end up in hospital beds in all marriages. And each one is different in its own way.' She looks at Sid and Aanya as if for support.

'We had our ups and downs—'

'*Had?* You're still married to Akbar Khan, aren't you?'

'I doubt he'll want to stay married to me when he returns, considering the unfortunate publicity the newspapers have given him since last week. And maybe it is time for me, too, to move on after this incident.'

'Oh OK, I get it now. So…what were you saying?'

'I said we had our share of ups and downs, but we had…have a rock-solid foundation, I'd say.' This time round I look at Aanya, then at Sid if they care to provide their point of view.

'As a matter of fact, we didn't know about any of this or Akbar's shortcomings. Everything seemed hunky-dory on the surface, honestly. Truth be told, we often even talked about them, Anush and Akbar, as being a perfect couple, didn't we?' Aanya puts forth the question to Sid.

'Certainly. And not just us. You can ask some of the other people who know them both and I am pretty sure their views will be congruous with ours.'

ACP Jha takes that in. Then: 'When did your husband start abusing you? Physically or mentally?'

I am agape. I am enraged. I can feel my neck flaming up. 'I don't like how you insinuate that abuse was a regular occurrence in our marriage, and I choose not to answer if that's all right with you.' I've had enough of her questions. 'Anything that happened, or happens, between Akbar and me is for Akbar and me to sort out. As you mentioned earlier, I'm still married to Akbar, he's still my husband and it would be a lot better if instead of questioning me about my relationship with my husband, you deployed your resources to find him, please.'

'Well, I can't force you to make a complaint against your husband, certainly not against a missing one. And I'm truly sorry, my intentions are not to deprecate you or your marriage in any way. I'm simply trying to get details to picture what frame of mind your husband might have been in.'

'How do you mean?'

'Well, even if – *if* – he has an abusive personality, he has certainly outdone himself this time, causing more harm to you than ever before. We've checked and there is no record of your injuries or hospital visits before this. As if that isn't bad enough, he shot dead his friend and business associate who also happened to be your boyfriend, and subsequently disappeared. Consequently, it is not beyond the police to surmise that he might decide never to return.'

'What about all the money?' Sid intervenes.

'Well, none of us has been able to establish how many accounts he holds under various names, apart from the two secret bank accounts we've uncovered so far. Mrs Khan, didn't you mention that you were an equal partner in two joint accounts?'

'Yes, as far as I know, I still am, unless he changed his instructions to the bank.'

'That's not possible without your consent. Once you've been added as a signatory, even if the account had originally only belonged to Akbar Khan, he cannot take that authority away without your consent.'

'That's true,' Sid endorses.

'How much money is there in those accounts, if I may ask?'

'I wouldn't know, certainly not off the top of my head,' I say. I know approximately, but I am not inclined to spell out the number in the presence of Aanya and Sid. If ACP Kamala wants to know, I'm sure she can take the legal route.

'Any guesses?' She's not someone who gives up easily. 'More than a few crores?'

I give a nearly imperceptible nod.

'Fifteen? Twenty?'

'Yeah, something like that,' I agree nonchalantly.

'That's a lot of money, don't you think?'

'This is just what was there. That's the reason I think there has to be some sort of misunderstanding. There was no incentive for Akbar to risk his reputation carrying out illegal activities to make any more money.'

Everyone looks at me. My voice, I realise, has gone up several octaves.

'Well, we will get to the truth, I promise you that, Mrs Khan. Meanwhile, I have a request, which I hope you won't decline, as I could really do with your help here.'

'Sure, what is it?'

'I'd appreciate it if you could accompany me to your house to take me through the events of last Saturday evening. Revisiting the scene isn't atypical, as it has been proven time and again that it aids in evoking memories in those who were present at the time of the incident. You might be reminded of something from the evening that's inadvertently escaped your memory or something you might have hitherto considered inconsequential.'

The three of us nod like puppets.

'We also cannot overlook the fact that you've been through severe trauma and hospitalisation,' she continues, '…and that isn't conducive to thinking straight. In fact, in my opinion, you might be suppressing the bad memories inadvertently or consciously trying to forget the whole experience. As such, minor details are lost. And believe me, nothing is trivial in a homicide investigation. No fact is small, irrespective of how impertinent it seems to you. While we are there, it will jog your memory, and I'll be much obliged if you could tell me everything and let me decide on including or excluding details in the investigation, please.'

'Of course.' At the very least, I will get to see my home. To know how it feels after it's been a scene of murder.

'Can we come along?' Sid asks.

'Ideally, I'd say no, but there is no point in me declining your request. You will call up someone high up in the ministry who will then call my boss and I'll be unofficially *told* to take you along, so I might as well say yes to your request now.' She smiles wryly. She is not happy about it.

'It's just that until Akbar is back, and we've had a word or two with him and everything has been sorted, we don't want Anush to feel alone. We feel responsible for her,' he explains.

'Thank you.' I've never experienced such a loyal friendship. To be honest I have little expectations of anyone else. Sid and Aanya are a godsend.

'When do you want Anush to be there?'

'As soon as possible really? The sooner we finish at the residence at Sainik Farms, the earlier Mrs Khan can get her house back. I'm sure that's what you want.'

'Of course.'

'How about tomorrow morning at nine? I can send a vehicle—'

'That's really not necessary. Anush is with us, and the three of us will see you there at nine.'

'Thanks, Mr Dhariwal. One more thing I want to ask before I go. Do you think anyone other than Akbar in your circle of friends might be involved in money laundering?'

'It's funny that you ask that. We discussed the same thing at lunch today. As far as I know, no one is. Rajiv was the only one who was rudderless – no wife, no family, not much money – and consequently, he might have been easily persuaded to join hands with Akbar—'

'You're saying that like you know it firsthand?'

'I'm not sure I follow you.'

'You are happy to believe that Akbar led Rajiv down the proverbial garden path and not the other way round.'

'It seems so.'

'In my experience, things are not always what they seem, Mr Dhariwal. What if Rajiv had access to the money laundering trade and he convinced Akbar to join him?'

'Well, we wouldn't know.'

'Exactly. I think I've taken enough of your time today. Just an update from my side – the search for Akbar and his car is still on, and I shall let you know if we discover anything. Meanwhile, if you remember anything that you think might be relevant, please don't hesitate to call me directly at any time, night or day.'

Twenty-Three

'Is it just me or do you both also get this feeling that the ACP has read too many Miss Marple mysteries?' Sid asks after Kamala leaves and he's fixed himself a drink. The amber liquid in his cut-glass tumbler is tempting, but I have doctor's orders to follow. If I were home alone I'd certainly have had at least one drink. Aanya, to her credit, has declined to have a drink to keep me company with my fresh lime soda. *'Oh, the dead do tell tales, Mr Dhariwal,'* he imitates the ACP's tone. 'How filmy is that!'

'She most definitely thinks *she is* Miss Marple, but I have a feeling she knows more than she's letting on, which is obviously her job. All this crap about Rajiv not returning home on Friday, and him – hypothetically – being with Akbar adds up to nothing. So what if they were together on Friday evening? Rajiv died on Saturday evening when he went to Sainik Farms. Anushka saw him arrive at her house before the fracas ensued. The police have evidence that Akbar called Rajiv on Saturday evening and that Rajiv took the call. The autopsy must have revealed the time of death as Saturday, not Friday, so what was she going on about? Does she think Akbar shot Rajiv on Friday evening, and then went about his business with Rajiv's corpse in the boot of his car for twenty-four bloody hours?'

'Impossible. Unless Rajiv was resurrected on Saturday evening, how did I see him alive? I know I did. What I don't know is where either of the two men were – together or independently – on the evening before.'

'I don't believe they were together,' Sid adds. 'Just think about it with a cool head. Akbar comes to know about Anush's affair with Rajiv. He either accepts it like a mature individual – although I can't see it, but let's assume he does – and values his friendship with Rajiv more than his infraction solely for business purposes, perhaps, and not only that: he also takes Rajiv out for drinks and dinner on Friday night.

'The alternative would be – and which resonates more with what really occurred afterwards – Akbar takes a firm stand and decides to cut Rajiv off from his personal and business life completely, calls him over on Saturday evening to talk and things turn ugly as we know they did. It can't be both. He can't be partying with Rajiv on Friday, and then call him over and shoot him on Saturday. It makes no sense, don't you agree?'

Sid's logic has no fractures. Miss Marple or not, in the back of my mind, I hear a creepy little voice of caution: *watch out. This ACP is casting the net wide.*

'We are missing a crucial piece here,' I say.

'Which is?'

'Who influenced Akbar to get into money laundering in the first place? I can't imagine Akbar woke up one morning and decided to go looking for people who run hawala…which means someone came with an offer to Akbar, and it was too lucrative for Akbar to refuse. I don't believe it was an unknown person. It has to be someone he knew and trusted, don't you think?'

'Now that you say that, it makes complete sense. We all agree he didn't *need* the money so maybe it started as "helping out a friend" and somehow never stopped since the returns were too good to forsake.'

'You sure know a lot about the returns from hawala,' Aanya jokes. 'Is that firsthand knowledge, Mr Dhariwal?'

Sid doesn't look amused. He turns and goes to the bar to make himself his fifth – or is it sixth? – drink. I see him pour three fingers into his glass, top it with soda and bring it back.

'Or,' he says, 'someone forced his hand.'

'How do you mean?'

'Someone made him an offer…'

'He couldn't refuse?' Aanya finishes off. 'Now who's being filmy, Don Corleone?'

'I'm being serious.'

'It is possible. Everyone knows Akbar has money and connections. That he has – or should I say, had – a great reputation as a nawab, a model citizen, as he donated a lot to charities, so who would think that a law-abiding philanthropist would get into the murky world of money laundering? He had a perfect façade.'

'I'm glad you said that, Aanya. If I had conceived and propagated this theory you'd have accused me again of having *firsthand* knowledge of how Akbar got into this illegal trade.'

'I didn't mean it that way, but you are hiding something, and I know that.'

I believe Aanya is correct. Sid's demeanour has slightly altered since the ACP slammed his hypothesis earlier. Anxiety shows on his face, in the increasing size of his drinks, and in his attempts at avoiding eye contact with either of us.

'What?'

'What are you not telling us, Sid?'

'Are you Miss Marple now?'

'That is not the answer to my question.' Aanya sounds grave. I feel guilty for being present there. The last thing I want is to cause discord between them. They live separate, independent lives, and the only bond that connects them is the trust between them. I don't want to be the one who creates a rift.

'OK, it was one time, just one time, I swear.'

'Good boy, Sid, good boy!' Aanya says in a high-pitched voice like she's rewarding a puppy for showing off his skills. 'What was just one time? Out with the truth now please, Mr Dhariwal.'

Twenty-Four

'I was desperate, I needed help and I didn't know who else I could fall back on, so I asked for a one-time favour,' Sid sounds hesitant.

Aanya says nothing, but I notice that her eyes are unblinkingly glued to his face, daring him to stop or prevaricate. As a married couple, they've always intrigued me – for lack of a more appropriate word or term – with their open version of marriage. For one, the coincidence of two business families arranging an alliance of their children, and that they are both gay makes it a second coincidence, enough to astonish you. More to the point, the two adapted their lifestyles to suit each other. No one else can guess the dynamics of their relationship. How do they accommodate each other's lovers? Does the fact that your spouse's lover is not a member of your own sex relieve you of all jealousy?

In the past, I have seriously pondered whether they already knew each other through their families and went into marriage knowing exactly what they'd do next.

'Oh, do you remember Charlie?' he asks.

'Remind me.'

'He was the violinist from Mumbai who came and stayed with us for two weeks about a year ago.'

'The time you told me to cancel all professional and social engagements because you both didn't come out of the bedroom the entire time?'

'That's the one.'

'What happened?'

'Well, he wasn't anything that he said he was. He wasn't a violinist, and he wasn't from Mumbai either; he was from Goa. He called me immediately after that trip, told me that he had been called for an interview in a renowned national magazine, and said that if I wanted him not to talk about me, I needed to pay him.'

'How much?'

'One crore – that was what he said the magazine was offering him to reveal names of homosexual industrialists.'

'And how did Akbar help you?'

'Charlie wanted cash to be delivered to him in Goa, and I went to Akbar for help.'

That surprises me. 'Why would you go to Akbar if you didn't know he was running a hawala shop?'

'I swear I didn't. I had gone to seek advice as a friend.'

'What happened?' Aanya takes over again.

'Well, he did help me. He told me he'd help me get the cash to Goa for a small fee.'

'That doesn't prove that Akbar shifted the money himself. It could be that he knew some hawala broker whom he must've paid to transfer the funds to Charlie in Goa.' I have no clue why I'm defending Akbar.

'That's what he told me he did. He also told me he'd ensure there were no problems and no one would ever know about the transaction. He said he'd send Rajiv.'

'Why didn't you tell me all this?'

'It was like a quid pro quo between friends, Aanya. He was saving my ass – how do you expect me to talk about it, giving away his secrets?'

'So Akbar knows you're gay?' Aanya asks.

Sid nods. Then: 'But I swear he doesn't know that you are. He doesn't know that we have an arrangement.'

'I think we've strayed too much from the imminent problem,' Aanya declares. 'I think the entire hawala thing has distracted us all. We and ACP Jha should be focusing on the murder of Rajiv and on finding Akbar. Whether Akbar is or was involved in anything illegal should be secondary. Shouldn't murder trump hawala?'

'I guess the ACP is looking at all possible angles,' I say softly. 'What could the other possible angles be?'

'Perhaps – and I'm not saying it happened, but if hawala was such a huge money-spinner for Akbar and Rajiv – what if Rajiv didn't arrive at our home alone last Saturday night? What if there was another person in the car outside, waiting…?'

'Waiting for what?'

'I don't know. I'm only theorising. I'm not saying there was someone, but what if there were?'

'Seriously?' Sid picks up on my uncertainty.

'I can't say. I'm simply speculating like the police. Jha broke the rules and came to see me in the hospital to convince me that Akbar might not be responsible for murder...Rajiv came to the door. I saw Rajiv, and no one else. I did not see anyone else that night, but that does not prove there wasn't anyone else around.'

'Do you think Akbar might have known there was someone with Rajiv?'

'Maybe Akbar knew, maybe he didn't, I wouldn't know.'

'Anush has a point, Aanya.'

Aanya and I look askance at Sid.

'It makes sense. If there was indeed a third person at the scene that night, what says it wasn't that unknown person who shot Rajiv and dashed?'

'And Akbar? Why did he have to disappear?'

'Out of fear? Shock? I mean he'd just seen his friend getting shot! For all we know, Akbar might have gone chasing this murderer and it didn't go down as well as expected—'

A guttural cry escapes my throat.

'Oh Anush, I don't mean Akbar has come to any harm, but nonetheless this theory needs to be fleshed out, wouldn't you agree?'

Aanya and I look at each other and nod. The theory is sound, but it's a theory.

'What are we having for dinner?' Aanya changes the topic.

'Let's go out tonight?'

'Anush might not want to go, so why don't we just order some food? Chinese or Italian?'

'Italian, please.'

SUNDAY, 14TH JULY

Twenty-Five

I've always been a morning person but even by my standards I'm up early today. It's just turned five and I'm up. I can't say I had a good night's sleep anyway. There's a lot hanging in the air, and I'm scared something might drop on my head. I had a dreadful night. Bad dreams. There was blood everywhere in one of them; in one, I was wearing the same pink sheath dress I wore that Saturday, but it was drenched in blood, soaking wet. I woke up several times and drank copious amounts of water. I guess my system is flushing out toxins. My phone is charged, so I am at least connected to the world. I think of Akbar, but it makes little sense to call him. His phone is with the police, it must have been pulled apart by forensics or data analysts to find any clues. I check the web – the news is full of Akbar's disappearance, Rajiv's homicide and me. To my astonishment, the coverage of me isn't as reprehensible as I had imagined. The tonality hints at pity rather than suggesting I'm a seductress or an adulteress.

The affair is mentioned, yes, but it's not the pivot; money laundering is the focus, for which I'm grateful. But I know the media can change tracks the minute they discover that Rajiv had candid photographs of me. Whatever sells best, isn't that what they say?

There's a knock on the door, and Aanya comes in holding two mugs of hot coffee. 'Good morning...did you sleep well?'

'Oh yes, it was quite comfortable,' I lie, not wanting to appear an ungrateful guest. 'What time do we have to leave?'

'It shouldn't take more than an hour from here even with the traffic so I think we should leave by eight. What will you have for breakfast?'

'I don't feel like—'

'That's not an option. How about soft-boiled eggs?'

I love eggs. Poached, boiled or fried, sunny-side up, and Aanya knows it. Omelettes and scrambled eggs are good dishes, but they never give me the satisfaction of devouring an egg.

'Yes, please.'

***

'We're almost there,' Sid says as we approach Sainik Farms. Travelling with the Dhariwals invokes memories that lay buried, of the last time I was in their car, still hazy from the drugs at the hospital. Sid and Akbar bought their cars on the same day – the Mercedes E200, black with black leather interiors. I remember that they negotiated a 20 per cent discount on the list price and also got some add-ons. It's funny how the mind stores such inconsequential bits of information to throw back at you when it's absolutely irrelevant. Or perhaps it is a kind of coping mechanism the brain has devised to preserve sanity at times when both your oars are out of the water.

My house – our home – looks deserted. Thankfully, there are no police tapes like in the movies but there are four uniformed police officers on the property. In case the neighbours had missed some news, they could always surmise from the police vehicles coming and going, maybe even stop one of the constables for the latest gossip.

There are no private cars on the drive; the police have taken away my car and Rajiv's. As we drive up to the house, the garden appears tended, thank God. So the gardener has been allowed in by the police – or the plants would be wilted and the grass yellowed by now. The police must have checked and cleared the garden, too. The curtains inside the house are drawn, like when we returned from holidays.

However, during those times the staff were present and the lights and air conditioning on. From a distance I spot ACP Kamala Jha in uniform standing confidently as though she owns the house and is present there to welcome us as the host. Her smile is astroturf, not real; I am increasingly becoming wary of this woman. Wary and tired of her behaviour, her methods and, most importantly, her stealth. Bloody drama queen.

'Good morning.' Sid's voice is honey-smooth. It appears he's trying to charm her. A stray thought flashes across my mind…have Sid and Kamala interacted before this investigation? If yes, why? How? When? They seem to be extremely comfortable with each other and it is not mutual attraction. It cannot be. Sid has no interest in women, I know that.

'And how are you this morning, Mrs Khan?' Kamala brings me back to the present.

'I'm good, thanks, and you?'

'Fine, fine. Let's go inside.'

My own house seems alien to me. The broad entrance hall, the console table on the right as you enter. The mirror above that, which is shattered, with blood stains still perceptible. There are no stains on the floor – they've been wiped off. I guess the crime scene investigators or forensics or someone else took samples and then cleaned the area.

We turn left from the foyer into our living-cum-dining room, which is the size of a mini tennis court. Everything here is as it was when I last saw it. Of course, the glasses that I left on the table are gone, presumably picked up by the police for prints.

'Where do we begin?' I love Sid. Akbar and I admired this often. He has the natural ability to start, lead, continue, shift and conclude any conversation.

'We are here for Mrs Khan to look, see and think if there's anything that reminds her of the events of the night in question.

'We know, but can I throw a spanner in your brilliant work so far, please?'

'Of course, go ahead.'

'We know from your investigation that both Akbar and Rajiv were involved in unsavoury dealings—'

'You mean hawala.'

'You're correct, ACP Jha.'

'Carry on.'

'If they were certainly – I say that with caution because I don't know; I'm going by what you've shared with us until now – involved in hawala, there could be other reasons why Rajiv is dead and Akbar is missing.'

Well played, Sid, I want to shout. You knew about hawala, you even laundered money using Akbar's services, but I keep my mouth shut. It's pointless to contradict him, to reveal we've discussed all this and more, at length, last night.

'Hmm...' is all the sound the ACP lets out.

'Think about it for a minute. It might sound as though I'm pontificating, but what if Rajiv had come with another man to see Akbar on the night in question? We don't know who this mystery man was or is, so let's just call him Mr X for the time being. Anush didn't see Mr X because whoever it was, he didn't come to the door, stayed in the background.'

ACP Jha looks amused, but she's a hard one to read. I can't figure out if she has any conviction in Sid's speculation whatsoever. Maybe she's merely humouring him.

'Yes, Akbar made a call to Rajiv, and that might have prompted the visit, but we still don't know the purpose of Rajiv's visit, do we? Perhaps it had to do with his affair with Anush, and he was there to blackmail Akbar; perhaps he was there for a hawala deal. In either scenario, it's not impossible to imagine he had brought someone along in case something were to go wrong...and things did go wrong, we know that.'

Kamala nods. I am standing on her side facing Sid, and I can't read her eyes.

'Something did not go as planned, that's for sure. Whatever it was that Rajiv wanted, Akbar certainly wasn't giving it to him. That might have led to an argument, which ended with one of them dead.' But Sid seemed to be really leaning into this new theory. 'What we don't know is what exactly conspired between the three of them that night—'

'Hold on a second, Mr Dhariwal, we haven't yet established that there were three people that night. There is no evidence of this mysterious Mr X that you have brought in from the cold.'

I was correct in my assessment: the ACP isn't buying Sid's story, which is hardly surprising.

'For instance,' ACP Jha says, 'if this was a misunderstanding or a fight between Akbar, Rajiv and this Mr X that you believe was present at the scene, why did Akbar try to throttle Mrs Khan and hit her head against the mirror? What wrong had she done?'

'What if it wasn't Akbar who pushed her head against the mirror?' How Sid pulls a wild card answer like that out of his hat every time, I'll never know.

'How do you mean?'

'Remember, Anush was drunk out of her senses, and also drugged, and so in the absence of any alternative she imagined that she was thrown against the mirror by Akbar—' Sid stands up and gesticulates holding an imaginary neck from behind and banging it against the wall. 'You cannot see whose hands they are from that angle…' He makes a valid point.

'But why do you think Akbar drugged Mrs Khan if there was no malicious intent?' ACP Kamala isn't swayed by Sid's hypothesis.

'Maybe Akbar wanted Anush to go to sleep, and not meet this mysterious Mr X.'

'And why, in your opinion, would he have done that?'

'I don't know, but I can guess.'

'Well, I can see that you can speculate extremely well, so why don't you tell us what your guess is?'

Is the ACP being sarcastic?

'Maybe there was a big business deal about to happen that Akbar didn't want Anush to know about. Maybe he was simply protecting her. He didn't know that things would escalate to an uncontainable level.'

'Hmm…hmm!'

'You see, Anush was out of her senses after the cocktail of drinks and drugs, so we can't fully trust what she remembers. Maybe she misremembers that Akbar was infuriated about her affair with Rajiv. That somebody pushed her against the mirror is evident – she had to be stitched up, the mirror is broken, the forensics have confirmed that the blood is hers – but for all we know, all this didn't go down the way Anush believes it did. Maybe the violence transpired only after Akbar saw that Rajiv had brought someone along.'

'But Mrs Khan saw her husband pull out his gun from the study,' Jha argues.

'Yes, and it had his fingerprints on it when you found it, I agree. But if this third person was wearing gloves, his prints wouldn't be on it. With Akbar missing you couldn't do a gunshot residue test to confirm if the gun was actually fired by him. Maybe the third person took the gun from Akbar and shot Rajiv, we don't know.'

I'm watching the story of my life, dramatised and narrated by others, from the sidelines.

'Well, if we believe there was a third unknown person that night, the entire dynamic changes.' The ACP appears to be coming around.

'Correct, ACP Jha. Perhaps there is a simpler explanation after all. Maybe it wasn't so much about Anush and Rajiv, but about some money deal.'

'Wait a minute, if we assume there was a third person in Rajiv's car who committed the murder and skedaddled, as you say – how did he get away? Because we found Rajiv's car here after the incident. If Mr X ran on foot, Akbar should have chased him on foot too.'

'Maybe Mr X did not travel in Rajiv's car.'

ACP Kamala turns to me. 'Mrs Khan, when you heard Rajiv arrive at your place did you hear the sound of one or two cars in your driveway?'

'Uhh...I honestly can't tell you even if my life depended on it, ACP Jha,' I tell her.

'So, this third man, this Mr X, drove off after shooting Rajiv, and Akbar drove after him?'

'Looks like it,' Sid sounds as confident as though he was present at the scene, had witnessed everything, and is now narrating the incident from memory.

'Where was Mr Khan's car parked?' ACP Jha asks me.

'I wouldn't know where he parked on that particular day. He usually parks in the garage, but sometimes he just leaves it on the driveway or right outside the garage.'

'For Akbar to give chase, it has to be on the driveway or he'd have lost precious time while Mr X got away.'

'Then, I'm sure it would have been parked on the driveway.' Sid's conviction is steadfast.

Twenty-Six

'It still leaves a lot of unanswered questions,' ACP Kamala Jha, considering her age, might seem inexperienced, but she isn't green. She hasn't betrayed any emotion. If she finds the theory of Mr X at our doorstep the other night bizarre she isn't letting her demeanour betray her thoughts. If she thinks Sid's entire narrative is impromptu – which, given he has nothing to substantiate his claims, probably is – she isn't dissecting it to make his hypothesis look like a dingleberry. She appears to be digesting all the info.

'It sure does,' Sid admits.

'Mrs Khan, didn't you say that your husband returned late on the night before the incident?'

'Yes.'

'When did you see him next?'

'Saturday morning. Akbar made coffee for the both of us and brought it into the bedroom to wake me up.'

'You told me earlier that he was taking some foreign clients out to dinner the night before, which turned out to be false, as we know. Did you two have any conversation in the morning regarding where he went, who he went with or how his evening went?'

'No.'

'And he didn't volunteer any details either?'

'No. Like I told you he had already informed me he'd be out with guests. This wasn't the first time he was out late on a business meeting so I saw no reason to suspect it wasn't true.'

'But this time he wasn't out on any work engagements as we have established. There were no guests from abroad. On the contrary, he left the office early that day. However, this is what the investigators found out from the people who work in his legitimate business. What none of us is privy to is whether Akbar had a second office in another location that we haven't discovered yet.'

I don't know how to respond to that.

'Which suggests he might have done this in the past too.' It's rhetorical. 'He must have another location from where he operated his hawala business. I can't picture large suitcases full of cash going in and out of his Barakhamba Road office and the staff there being ignorant of it, don't you think?'

'It is entirely possible that he used the same space after hours or over the weekends,' Sid says.

'But he went to the office last Saturday, and his staff was there so they definitely work on Saturdays…' ACP Jha looks at me expectantly.

'Every alternate Saturday,' I fill in. 'Akbar's staff works every alternate Saturday because trading takes place mostly on weekdays, it's only on weekends that they can tally the accounts and balances.'

'Makes sense,' the ACP acknowledges. 'Mr Dhariwal, do you have any insights you aren't sharing with us?'

'What do you mean?' This is the first time I have seen Sid flustered.

'You seem to believe that illegal business can be carried out of perfectly legal office set-ups after office hours, so I'm thinking maybe you know more than you're letting on.'

'It was just a thought.'

From the corner of my eye I can see Aanya glaring at her husband. She has, much like me, worked out that the 'one-time' Sid laundered money, it was likely at Akbar's office. Late in the evening or over a weekend.

'Hmm...' she says, which doesn't indicate whether she's falling for Sid's lie or not. Either way, ACP Jha is someone to be wary of. She can't be trusted, that much is obvious to me. She is astute – the manner in which she had so casually dropped by my hospital room for a chat to convince me to lie – she is sharp, she is cool with her responses. You cannot gauge how she perceives any of this. Oh, she's someone I'd be very careful of. There's no telling what she's thinking right now. Conceptualising and assembling a theory that I, or for that matter, Aanya and Sid, have no idea of.

'So, Mrs Khan, after your husband – or if we presume that Mr Dhariwal's hypothesis is correct and that you don't know who it was – pushed your head against the mirror so hard that it broke the glass and cut your skin and you fell from its impact, what happened next? Take me through the steps, please.' Her voice is calm, her words neutral, and it's impossible to detect if she's being sarcastic about Sid's theory of Mr X or if this is simply her manner of speaking – circumspect and rational about anything presented without tangible evidence.

'It took me a minute to gather myself. It had all happened in a flash, I didn't know what had happened until I was on the floor. I was scared, disoriented. My head was spinning; I could feel the pain but at the time, I had no idea I had a laceration that would require stitching up. Frightened, I ran towards my bedroom—'

'Any specific reason why you made a dash to the bedroom?' She looks towards the end of the foyer where my bedroom is. 'I mean, you had just come out of the living room before the attack so why didn't you rush back in?'

'I don't know. Somehow, it felt safer since I knew I could lock myself in.'

'And you thought you needed the security of a lock because...?'

'I thought Akbar might chase me...'

'But he didn't chase you. Not right away anyway.'

'But Anush didn't know that.' Sid cannot keep quiet.

'Mrs Khan, at the time, you didn't know there was a third person, so there was no rational reason for you to think Akbar would run after you to harm you, because if he had, Rajiv would have come after Akbar to save you, considering he had just witnessed your husband being violent.'

'I don't know what I was thinking, really.'

'Or maybe you knew there was a third person, and you comprehended the others were under attack, so...you tried to escape to save your life, leaving Akbar behind to fight his own battles because he was the one involved in illegal business, not you.' ACP Jha maintains a deadpan expression as she says it. Admittedly, her nonchalant façade is disquieting.

'ACP Jha, are you in any manner insinuating that Anush knew Akbar was involved in laundering money?' Aanya has stepped into the conversation.

'I am merely hypothesising like Mr Dhariwal here,' ACP Jha responds apathetically and moves on. 'Mrs Khan, when you called the police from inside the bedroom, you said your husband was at the door...'

'I'm not sure now, to tell you the truth. I had been violently assaulted, I'd made a run to the other side of the house, I was in a state of disarray. Drunk and – as I later found out – drugged. Then I heard a gunshot. Moreover, I was on the call with the police, so my attention must've been divided. I heard the loud banging on the door, and considering I had no idea that there might have been a third man in the house that night, I had no reason to doubt that it was anyone but Akbar at the door.'

'I can understand,' ACP Jha finally lets a sympathetic smile appear on her face. 'I've spoken to your staff once, Mrs Khan, but in light of this new premise, I'll have to see them again.'

'But...how will the staff know who came to Anushka's house on Saturday night when they weren't present?'

'Leave that to me, Mrs Dhariwal.'

Twenty-Seven

'Some cheek that woman has to simply drop by your hospital room, expect you to lie and set a trap for Akbar. What a bitch! You should have told her to get out of the room right away and give Piyush a call. Isn't it Piyush?'

Monica is a complete contrast to ACP Kamala when it comes to emoting feelings. She is beside herself, colour rising up her neck, when I narrate the events of the past few days. She's unhappy to begin with, as I had gone to Aanya's house from the hospital despite her making me an offer first. She called Aanya this morning when we returned from our visit to Sainik Farms and convinced her that I should spend today with Piyush and her. I will return to Aanya's tomorrow. No one asked for my opinion; I wasn't asked or consulted. I feel like a nomad moving from one friend's house to another, but a happy and wanted one.

'Of course, I'd have knocked some sense into her.'

'Sid took care of it, so it's OK,' I say. I give them details of how helpful Aanya and Sid have been, staying with me during the visits by the ACP, and even driving with me to my residence when the police asked me to visit the scene of the crime.

'So Sid came up with this alternative theory of an unseen Mr X?' Piyush has an impish smile on his face.

'Yes.'

'The Dhariwals appear to be quite invested in the case, I must say. If I'm right Sid pulled strings to visit the scene of the crime even before it was cleared by the police.'

'Don't be ridiculous, Piyush. He's only trying to be proactive, to help Anush...and Akbar,' Monica tells him.

'Oh I have no doubt he's being proactive. *Why*, is the fucking question...why is he trying to interfere and divert the investigation to save Akbar's ass now, when he knew all along that Akbar was involved in hawala.'

'Did you know?'

'Everyone who knows Akbar knows he was involved, directly or indirectly.'

'I didn't,' I say emphatically.

'I didn't either, so who does *everyone* comprise of?' Monica is grilling Piyush now.

'OK, I might have exaggerated. Not everyone. But anyone who has ever moved cash knows Akbar could get it done. He always claimed he knew someone who knew someone who was a hawala broker – the usual baloney – but it was pretty evident that he was doing it himself. I've transferred cash abroad a few times myself and frankly, I don't give a rat's ass if Akbar did it or if he used a third party as long as my money was safely delivered. The fact that Akbar was involved gave me the confidence to go through with the transaction.'

'You transferred money illegally?'

'Oh, don't act holier-than-thou please, Monica. Hawala isn't endemic, it's a worldwide arrangement of transferring cash from one place to another. I wasn't sending money for any illegal purpose, just moving some undisclosed money and saving on banking costs. And I'm being candid here, admitting it because it's only you and Anush here. I'm not going to acknowledge that I knew about Akbar's hawala dealings if questioned by the police, so don't expect me to come forward about anything regarding this. I don't want to get involved.'

'I can't imagine why Akbar had to do it – I mean his background, his status—'

'You're missing the point, Anush…it was his status and background that made him a strong contender. You need to be able to trust someone to hand over a few crores in cash to someone and not ask for a receipt. What if he disappeared? Akbar brought that trust and legitimacy to the entire thing with élan. And before you ask, Rajiv was in it solely for the money.'

So Piyush knew about Rajiv's involvement too. Silence ensues, neither Monica nor I have any arguments or questions. Piyush makes hawala sound legitimate, as though there's nothing wrong with it, and as if we and the police are making an unnecessary fuss.

'So you see why I think Sid is attempting to sabotage the police investigation?'

'He is not obstructing, he's only helping—'

'Really, Monica? The entire hypothesis of this unknown, invisible third person at Anush's residence on Saturday night is fucking bullshit if you ask me.'

'You have got to be kidding me,' I join the husband–wife argument. 'Why would Sid be lurking outside the house if he were present that night?'

No response. Piyush just shrugs.

'How well did you know Rajiv?' I ask.

'Well, don't speak ill of the dead and all that, but honestly, I had no time for that man, Rajiv Pant. I tolerated him for the sake of Akbar because they were buddies from school, and it didn't hurt to be polite. Didn't you ever feel that he was a sleazeball?' he asks both of us.

I know that now, and it was a tragic mistake I made, I want to say. 'I don't know.'

'I'm sorry, Anush, I didn't mean to put you on the spot,' Piyush backtracks. For a moment, it appears he might have forgotten about my relationship with Rajiv. 'Really sorry.'

'It's OK.'

'If you ask me,' Piyush cannot shut up, 'it went down exactly like the police originally said. Akbar came to know that Rajiv and you...' – he doesn't say the words – '...or maybe that idiot tried talking to Akbar about you, and when he turned up at your residence that night, Akbar lost it completely, and I don't blame him. After shooting Rajiv, he must've panicked. My guess is when he came banging on the bedroom door, his intention was not to shoot you, but to take you along with him—'

'Where?' I ask. 'Where would we go? It would have been impossible for both of us to hide when the police came looking for us.'

'I can take a guess at what Akbar might have wanted to do.'

'And what is that?'

'Akbar might not have wanted to run away that night. If you hadn't called the police, they wouldn't have arrived at your door within an hour. Your staff wasn't due in until Monday morning, giving the two of you enough time to think, plan, maybe dispose of Rajiv's body, clean up the mess and no one would have known—'

'What have you been drinking? Have you totally lost it now, husband dear?'

'It wouldn't be the first time someone went missing in Delhi and it won't be the last either. Even if Rajiv hadn't returned for a few days, the police wouldn't have jumped to the conclusion that he was dead and buried somewhere. When reported by neighbours, they'd have lodged a missing-person complaint, maybe superficially looked for him, but with Rajiv having no family, who would have hankered after the police? The enquiry would have lost its momentum even before it commenced. Think about it.'

Of course not, I know for certain. When the police discovered my candid photographs while searching his apartment, they'd have come straight to our house. Fortunately, the police have kept that discovery from the media and Monica and Piyush don't know about them yet.

'If only you had cooperated with Akbar—'

'Shut up, Piyush. Don't even suggest it's Anush's fault.' Monica sounds shocked at Piyush's behaviour. 'You've seen what Akbar did to her. How was she to know what his intentions were? And expecting Anush to cooperate in hiding a dead body? God, I never thought you were so twisted.'

'I was merely hypothesising, like our friend Sid.'

'At least Sid's theory is decent.'

'Or maybe it isn't a fucking theory at all.'

'What do you mean?'

'Could we talk of something else, please?' I plead. I neither have the patience to hear any more of Piyush's conjectures nor am I in any mood to entertain him so bluntly accusing Sid of involvement in Rajiv's murder or in Akbar's disappearance.

Piyush storms out of the room as if I'm the one propagating the weirdest of speculations.

'Sorry, Anush. Piyush doesn't mean a word he says. I think we are all upset by the events of the past week.'

I wish I had stayed back at Aanya and Sid's place. I decide that's what I'll do from now on until I get my house back. I've had enough presumptions for a lifetime.

MONDAY, 15TH JULY

Twenty-Eight

'I'm sorry, Anush, I couldn't visit you in the hospital as I was out of town.' Vasu has come by this evening. His name is Raghav Vasudev, but everyone calls him Vasu.

Last evening, after dinner, after we called it a day at Monica's, I called Aanya and told her to pick me up this morning. I was feeling claustrophobic at Monica's home. It was Piyush's behaviour that irked me. His bluntness was bordering on impertinence, and the accusations! To think that everyone and their pets were aware that Akbar was into money laundering with no evidence to support it was preposterous too. He laughed at Sid for advocating that there might have been a third person present at our house on the night of Rajiv's murder. He talked down to Sid. He spoke very disparagingly of Rajiv. I don't think it was one particular thing or even his being contemptuous towards any single individual that annoyed me; it was the sum of his lack of respect for everyone. I got the feeling that he didn't particularly want me at his place but had succumbed to Monica's insistence and invited me over.

Vasu on the other hand was a welcome sight. He is married to Jaya. They, too, were Akbar's friends from before I arrived in Delhi. Vasu is older than most in the group. He's tall and lean with a head full of curly hair that can shame any standard poodle. Jaya is – for lack of a better word – a sexpot. Dark, husky, petite and always underdressed, in my opinion. A siren. Aanya has told me that Jaya wasn't keen to see me in light of the current events, and Vasu is here to make up for it because he thinks otherwise. He had wanted to come and see me in the hospital earlier but had surrendered to Jaya's bidding, not wanting marital discord over visiting me. Honestly, it hardly matters.

Every single one of us has our compulsions and *majbooris*. Vasu is here now, and he's decided to let his curly hair down. He's staying over at the Dhariwals'. A sleepover.

What surprises me, however, is that he's bisexual, Aanya confided in me. So...he's not here to spend a night with *us,* he's here to spend 'quality time' with Sid. Aanya also told me that Jaya has no clue about Vasu's predilection for men. How can a wife not know, I wonder, but it's not for me to ponder. To be honest, I didn't know Aanya and Sid were so openly promiscuous in each other's presence, inviting their dates home. Then again, I should be the last person who should have any qualms about promiscuity. Perhaps I was too harsh in judging my mother at the time. But maybe, as Dylan so rightly said, '*the times they are a-changing*' now.

'Did the police find anything?'

'Nothing except what we told you already.'

'So it's you who is filling in the gaps?' Vasu asks Sid but looks at me.

'Seems like we are running a parallel enquiry.'

'And Piyush isn't very happy with that.' Don't ask me why I blurt this out, but I do. Maybe I'm frustrated beyond the point of caring. Yesterday was miserable if I have to be truthful – Piyush's attitude, his venomous stance towards everything happening in my life.

'WHAT?' I'm surprised it's Aanya and not Sid who reacts to my comment.

'Why?'

'He thinks,' I explain, 'that by proposing these alternatives, we are, in some warped way, jeopardising the police investigation.' I give them a summary of my discussion without mentioning that Piyush accused Sid of being *the Mr X* in his own story. That, I know, will prompt a phone call right now and the conversation will not have a happy ending.

'And why will the policewoman be at all receptive to our theories if they sound so outlandish?'

'I have no idea why Piyush thinks what he thinks.'

'I'll tell you why. He disregards every word I say because I'm different,' says Sid.

'How do you mean?'

'He knows I'm gay so...everything I say means something entirely different to him. It's like I speak a foreign language. Most of the time, he is snobby with me, even at parties. Let me ask you this: have you ever seen the two of us together at a party, chatting?'

I try to remember, but I can't think of a single occasion at our place or anyone else's where I saw Piyush and Sid standing in a corner, having a conversation on their own. However, that doesn't mean anything. I haven't seen Vasu alone in the corner chatting to Sid either. My not seeing something does not establish that it hasn't ever occurred. Nevertheless, I appreciate Sid's point of view because I know Piyush has a conceited and ultraconservative view of life. He is someone who believes things need to be done the way his grandmother used to do them. I bet his grandmother didn't fucking use foul language. Well, I am not here to change the world.

'Well,' Vasu bridges the gap in the conversation, 'if the policewoman thinks it is a credible enough alternative, then I'm with Sid – the police must look into it as something plausible before ruling it out altogether.'

'Oh certainly.'

'But you have no idea who it could have been?' Vasu asks me.

'I honestly don't—'

'To be fair, Anush had no idea that Akbar was involved in high-value hawala transactions either,' Sid points out.

'Well, I can't blame her. I didn't know that either until I read about it in the papers.'

'I have a feeling this will blow over if we just keep calm,' Sid says as he makes another round of drinks for the two of them. Aanya isn't drinking; she's keeping me company as I am still following the doctor's orders, being careful about what I eat and drink.

'What if...' Vasu says, 'there's another angle to all this...?'

'Go on.'

'What if Rajiv brought someone to Akbar and Anush's house that night, but this Mr X double-crossed him?'

'Sorry,' I say. 'I don't follow you.'

'OK, let me elaborate. The third guy, as Sid pointed out, might have been there at your door that Saturday evening. In all probability, Mr X travelled to Sainik Farms with Rajiv in his car. He was supposed to – or at the very least that's what Rajiv believed – assist Rajiv in bringing down Akbar in some way that we don't know of yet. However, Akbar was aware that Mr X would be coming with Rajiv…because this Mr X double-crossed Rajiv and teamed up with Akbar…are you with me?'

All of us nod, although I haven't the faintest idea where Vasu is leading us with his convoluted conjecture.

'It all begins to add up, doesn't it?' he asks.

'What does?' Sid asks.

'If Akbar had known Rajiv intended to be difficult by bringing Mr X to the door, who was now in cahoots with Akbar, then it was logical that Akbar didn't want Anush to be around when the two men arrived at his door.'

'So is that why he plied me with drinks and drugs?'

'I can't think of any other reason. Pardon my insolence, but if Akbar had any inkling that you were involved with Rajiv, he wouldn't want you around when they took Rajiv down. Akbar couldn't forcibly throw you out of the house or find an excuse to send you away or lock you in the garage, Anush, so the only viable option he had left was to lace your drinks with drugs so you didn't witness or remember anything. Of course, the timing did not work in his favour. If it had been another thirty minutes, you'd have passed out, and maybe…just maybe, the plan was to move Rajiv's body out, but you called the police before Akbar and Mr X could do that, leaving them with no alternative but to go on the run.'

We all look at each other, agape.

'Just to confirm, what you're suggesting, Vasu, is that Rajiv did not get killed because of an impromptu argument that flared up, but this was a planned, cold-blooded murder?' Sid asks.

'I'm saying that it is a strong possibility, and it cannot, and should not, be overlooked, considering the circumstances, whether or not there was a third person at Akbar and Anush's residence that day.'

'I can't believe Akbar is a cold-blooded murderer.' I'm seconds away from breaking down. My voice comes out choked.

'And I don't blame you for that. And I'm not suggesting we tell the police this theory, but you'll have to agree that it isn't impossible to believe.'

'It does make some sense, yes,' Aanya agrees, then puts her hand on my arm to comfort me.

It doesn't ring true at all to me, but I decide to keep my counsel to myself. Sometimes it's better to keep your mouth shut, like they say.

And then my mobile starts to ring, which it hasn't done in the last seven days.

Twenty-Nine

'Mrs Khan?'

Instant recognition. It's ACP Kamala Jha. My mind goes into turmoil. It's almost eleven at night. To receive a call from the police officer at this hour means she isn't looking for an answer to her Scrabble puzzle. This has to be serious.

'Yes, it is. What is it, ACP?'

'Do you know of any other office or residence that Rajiv Pant owned across Delhi or in the NCR?'

'No.'

'None?'

'None whatsoever.'

'Hmm...strange.'

'Why do you ask?'

'He bought a large deep freezer a week before his death...and we didn't find it at his residence so I was wondering if, by chance, you knew of any other place he might have installed it?'

'No, I really don't know. How big was this freezer?'

'Quite large.'

'In that case, if it was large, it makes me think that he wouldn't have driven home with it in his car's boot. So, someone would have delivered it somewhere, if not to his apartment.'

'I must say, you make a good point, Mrs Khan.'

'If you find the address it was delivered to, you will find the location…but…may I know why a freezer bought by Rajiv has any relevance to my husband's disappearance?'

'The short answer is, I don't know, Mrs Khan, but I am on it. Are you still staying with the Dhariwals?'

'Yes.'

'We should be able to get you into your residence by this weekend, I promise.'

'Thank you.'

'Thanks for your time, Mrs Khan.'

'What was she after?' Aanya asks the moment I get off the phone. She has already guessed who I was speaking to.

'The ACP wanted to know if Rajiv had another property in the city, owned or rented.' I tell them what she was looking for.

'A freezer?'

'Yes.'

'Maybe Rajiv was planning on starting an ice cream business because he realised his paintings were pure crap.' Sid lets out a chuckle. 'You were right to ask how it is relevant, Anush.'

'Well, depending on its size – and I am playing the devil's advocate here – a freezer she described might be large enough to hold a corpse,' Vasu says.

'You're such a charmer, aren't you?'

'I said I was playing the devil's advocate. I'm not saying that's what it was, but it is possible.'

'It is possible because, truth be told, hypothetically everything is possible,' I tell him off tersely. 'That does not mean it's probable or that it ever happened. What do you think happened? Rajiv bought a freezer a week before his death. Then, according to your theory, Akbar sided with Mr X, shot Rajiv and then the two of them ran and hid themselves inside this freezer?'

'I'm sorry.'

'I'm sorry too, for my reaction.' I realise I've rebuked him a little too harshly.

'All of these theories make some sense individually, but they make little sense when we put them together.'

'You're correct, Sid. I think the police are clutching at straws. They have nothing to go on. A freezer bought by Rajiv – for all we know he donated one to charity or gave it as a gift to one of the galleries that host his worthless art.'

'The fact still remains that he bought one and the police cannot find it,' Aanya adds.

'The ACP isn't wrong to investigate as it strongly suggests Rajiv had another place – a house, a flat or a workshop.' She looks at me. 'And if there is one, and if Akbar knew about it, he might be there now.'

I shake my head. 'If he did, I don't know.' Does she think Rajiv bonked me on top of a freezer?

'Don't you all find it ludicrous that this policewoman thinks it important to find a freezer purchased by our friend Rajiv, and she doesn't go after a missing car?' Vasu seems to have a point. 'I mean...a car is worth more, should have greater visibility, especially a black E-Class Mercedes, so where is it? Shouldn't that be her prime objective? To locate the damn car? Or am I being unrealistic?'

'No, not at all,' Sid agrees.

'I need a drink,' I say.

'You are not allowed to consume alcohol, isn't that what the doctor said?' Aanya points out.

'What do you mean *allowed*? Anush is an adult, and while I appreciate what the doctor recommends, she is free to—'

'Shut up, Vasu,' Aanya scolds him, but it's one of those frivolous, friendly nags. 'I'm the one abstaining here with Anush.'

***

The dinner is mutton biryani. Honest, sumptuous food. It is hard to resist, but I only take a small portion and fill my stomach with mango kulfi later.

'Where could Akbar have gone?' Since Sid and Vasu have taken the second guest room in their house, Aanya and I are drinking hot chocolate in bed when she brings up Akbar. She asked me before dinner if she could stay the night with me rather than in her bedroom. I didn't probe, but I assumed it might be difficult if your spouse had another bed partner for a sleepover irrespective of how open your relationship might be.

'I know it sounds foolish, but I almost want him to slip up just once, so the police can know his direction of travel. It might not be good for him in the long run, but I want to know that he's safe, wherever he is…'

'Why would he be unsafe?'

'I don't know. We don't know if there was a third person and who this third person, Mr X, was, and we don't know the reason he was at our home in the first place. We have no idea if he is dangerous, if Akbar followed him and got into trouble or if he was Akbar's accomplice. In any event, how can the two of them just disappear?'

'I don't think they've disappeared; I think they are somewhere in or around Delhi in a safe house—'

'Aanya, *safe house* is a term I've read about in books and seen used in Hollywood films. If there is such a house that Akbar's gone to, there has to be some record of a property bought, leased or rented by him. Surely, I'd have known if he had another place, don't you think?'

'You may have a point, but what if this safe house is owned or rented by Mr X? How would you know about that?'

'I wouldn't. And until the police find out who this Mr X is, they cannot find the place either.'

'You're right. I think the ACP should be focusing on identifying Mr X, not looking for a freezer Rajiv bought a week before his death. I'll try and tell her tomorrow that she should stop wasting time looking for a freezer and focus on the identity of Mr X.'

TUESDAY, 16TH JULY

Thirty

ACP Jha is at the door at eleven in the morning. Sid has left for work, and Aanya has stayed home to keep me company.

'Have you found Akbar or identified Mr X?' Aanya asks as she lets Kamala into the living room.

'Not yet.'

'But you see, it's vital to identify Mr X. Two grown men can't vanish into thin air. They have to be somewhere. If Akbar had another place to stay, Anush would have known. I am pretty sure this place where Mr X has taken Akbar is not owned by him. We find who Mr X is, we find his place, we solve the case.'

'I'm sorry, Mrs Dhariwal, but I have to remind you I am the lead investigator in this case. There is no *we*. I can't burn manpower and valuable resources on baseless conjectures. I need tangible evidence. The existence of Mr X itself is conjectural, not even circumstantial. I'm sorry, but I would really appreciate it if you would let me run the investigation, please.' This is the first occasion the ACP has been uncompromisingly assertive. She has almost dismissed Aanya. 'Mrs Khan, I have a few questions, if I may.'

'Of course.'

'The freezer, the one Rajiv Pant purchased exactly a week before his death, do you know anything about it?' she asks again.

'Absolutely not. The first I heard about it was from you last evening. How should I know why Rajiv purchased a freezer of all things? And more to the point why should he tell me? Anyway, who told you about this freezer Rajiv bought and how is it relevant to the case?'

'We got details from his credit card company, which told us all the activity on his credit card in the last couple of months. The freezer stood out because it was a big-ticket item and we did not find it in his apartment.'

'He might have bought it for someone else. For a charity, perhaps?' Aanya suggests. 'We found the merchant he bought the freezer from and one of my team members gave them a visit this morning. You were correct, it couldn't have been carried by Rajiv in his car so he arranged for a delivery.'

'That's it. It's at Mr X's residence—'

'No, Mrs Dhariwal, it wasn't delivered to Mr X's residence,' the ACP interrupts Aanya and glares at me. 'Rajiv asked for the freezer to be delivered to your residence at Sainik Farms.'

'WHAT? Are you serious?'

'I am, and the van delivered it to your residence three days after the purchase date.'

'I don't believe it.'

'Surely, if the freezer was delivered to Anush's residence, she would have known that.'

'That's exactly what I think.'

'But why would Rajiv order a freezer and get it delivered to our place? Akbar and I never even discussed buying a large freezer, and if we needed one we'd have bought it ourselves. What use would a freezer be for Akbar or me?'

'Your guess is as good as mine,' ACP Jha says. Then, 'Mrs Khan, what I find rather strange is that while you look quite intelligent and observant to me now, you've been – deliberately or inadvertently – quite oblivious to whatever was happening around you.' Her eyebrows are raised like she's asking me a question.

'How do you mean?' Aanya asks her.

But the ACP is looking directly at me when she responds. 'For example, you tell me that you weren't aware that your husband was involved in money laundering, which is something I have a hard time accepting. I mean you are a couple, married long enough, living under the same roof—'

'I had no clue, I swear.'

'So you say.'

'You don't believe me?'

'Quite frankly, I don't know you well enough to make that call, Mrs Khan. We met last week, and not under the most normal circumstances, so I can't decide if I should believe you until I have further evidence.'

***

'Outrageous, bloody bitch, who does she think she is talking to?' Aanya seems to have lost control of her vocal cords. Sid has returned after lunch and she has poured herself a gin and tonic. She tells Sid that the police haven't identified Mr X, and the sense she and I got from Kamala was that they weren't serious about finding him either.

'There is a gaping hole in their investigation then,' Sid says.

'She was downright rude and condescending when I mentioned it to her. She practically told me to shut up and let her carry on the investigation her way. Then, she told Anush that she either knew about Akbar's hawala business or she's dumb.' Aanya looks at me for corroboration.

I give a slight nod.

'Anush didn't know about Akbar's illegal business.'

'How do you know?'

'Because Akbar told me when he helped me that one single time. He made me promise that the information should never be shared with Anush. "She should never come to know about this," I remember his precise words.'

'So why are you breaking the promise now?'

'Well, with one dead body and Akbar missing, a promise made in good times hardly stands its ground.'

'Can you tell that to ACP Jha?' I ask.

'Tell her what?'

'Tell her that you know I didn't know about Akbar's money-laundering business.'

'I hear what you're saying, but accepting that Akbar told me not to mention it to you also confirms that I knew about it, which will put us under unnecessary scrutiny. We love you, and we want to help, but the last thing I want is the police and the taxman snooping around, asking us for our accounts and records of business transactions. We cannot afford that.'

He needs to save his skin. Self-preservation is a natural instinct.

'Sid has a point,' Aanya furthers his explanation. 'Besides, it doesn't matter if you knew about hawala or not, you weren't involved in the murder of Rajiv, the disappearance of Akbar or anything to do with this unknown, as yet unidentified, Mr X.'

'Trust me, I didn't know about all this money laundering...' Tears start rolling down my cheeks. I sincerely hope my friends believe me.

'Obviously, we trust you.' Aanya is almost in tears too.

'And what did she say after she told you the freezer was delivered to your place?' Sid wants to know.

'Nothing. The conversation segued into Akbar's hawala, hinting that Anush isn't telling her everything.'

'You're correct, I find this ACP's tactics quite weird too.'

'She's definitely not telling us something, Sid. You must call someone higher up to figure out what's going on before this ACP makes a five-course meal of this inquiry.'

'Sid, among other things, Piyush also told me that everyone who knew Akbar knew about his money-laundering side-business. Is that true?' I ask.

'I don't think so. I mean if everyone was aware how is it that he could carry on doing it? Hawala is best done in secrecy, it's not advertised on billboards.'

'But if what Piyush says is true, then it is possible that the police got scent of it, and Akbar would have had to disappear regardless of Rajiv's murder. What choice did he have left?'

'You have a point there, Anush. With that being the case, I'd say he hasn't gone missing by chance, that this wasn't an impromptu escape, but more a carefully planned manoeuvre. But Rajiv's murder causes a rather intricate problem: how does that fit into all this?' Sid sounds contemplative.

'One more thing,' I say. 'What if neither Akbar nor Rajiv had invited Mr X that evening, and he slipped in quietly after Rajiv drove into our gates? And then Mr X intervened, managed to overpower Akbar, take the gun and shoot Rajiv, leaving Akbar with no other option but to run for his life.'

'So Sid wouldn't be wrong in his assumption that the person who knocked on your bedroom door might not have been Akbar, he might have been gone by then,' Aanya adds.

'The question still remains: if Akbar isn't involved in the murder, why hasn't he come forward until now? Where is he?'

'You mean something's happened to Akbar?' I break down now.

'Anush,' Aanya says and comes to sit next to me on the sofa, putting her arm around my shoulders as I sob.

Thirty-One

'We spoke to your staff, Mrs Khan.' ACP Jha is back in the evening. In her mission to crack this case, this policewoman seems to be all over the place. Why can't she ask all her questions in one go rather than dropping in twice a day? And to compound my misery she insists on meeting in person and not talking on the phone.

'And what did they have to say?' Sid asks. ACP Jha might have been indignant when Aanya intervened in the morning, but she doesn't show impatience with Sid. Maybe she knows who in this household is connected to the political world.

'Well, exactly like Mrs Khan had mentioned; all three of them had left your house on Friday evening, so they gave us nothing new. However, your gardener came on Saturday morning, and we managed to speak to him. According to—'

'Gururaj.' I can see she's struggling to remember the name.'

'Yes, thank you. According to Gururaj, Akbar's car was not in the driveway on Saturday morning at around eleven o'clock when he came to tend your garden.'

'Then it must have been in the garage, like I told you,' I remind her. 'Akbar made coffee for me and brought it into the bedroom. Without getting into details, we stayed in bed until noon and then we came out for lunch which had been prepared by the cook before he finished work on Friday evening. We microwaved the food and ate it in the kitchen itself.'

'And you did not step outside the house on that day for anything?'

'No.'

'Is that normal?'

'It wasn't either normal or unusual. It just so happened that I didn't need to step out at all. If I remember correctly, Akbar didn't venture out on that Saturday either.'

'Are you sure Akbar's car was in the garage then?'

'No. Our garage isn't integrated, it's not accessible from inside the house so there's no way I can confirm if the car was parked in it.'

'Could you see it from the window if it was parked outside?'

'Not necessarily. Akbar sometimes parked the car right in front of the garage, which isn't in sight if you're inside the house unless you go into Akbar's study and crane your neck to look for it.'

'That much I can vouch for,' Sid supports me, thankfully. 'Akbar parked it right in front of the garage at times.'

'If no one saw Akbar's car outside the house on Saturday, we can safely assume it was parked inside the garage. That being the case, it seems a bit surreal to imagine that he opened the garage, took his car out, and then had enough patience to close the garage and lock it before going away with this third person, Mr X, don't you think?'

'As a matter of fact, I do, but I have another theory.'

'Do tell, Mr Dhariwal.' If there is sarcasm in her voice I cannot tell.

'What if both Akbar and Rajiv were ignorant of Mr X being present that day until it was too late?' Sid presents my theory

– that the third man sort of jumped on both Akbar and Rajiv – as his own now, but I let him. I glance at ACP Jha and I can't confirm if she's buying it or not. She should be playing high-stakes poker at a casino.

'Well, that's interesting,' she says when Sid finishes. He has, I realise, embellished my suggestion with missing details: *Akbar might have had a gun, but he had no experience of using it. The gun might have been pulled out by Akbar only when he realised Rajiv and his life were in danger. If Mr X could push me (Anush) so hard against the mirror, he was certainly a lot stronger and tougher than both Akbar and Rajiv together.*

'But it raises further questions,' the ACP doesn't seem convinced.

'What other questions?'

'If Akbar saw Rajiv getting shot, he should've stayed back to protect his wife, and not run away.'

'Maybe he thought Mr X was not a danger to Anush since she wasn't involved in any way.'

'Then Akbar thought wrong. Someone did knock at Mrs Khan's bedroom door while she was reporting the incident to the police. I've heard the recording and I can hear loud and aggressive banging at the door in the background.'

'Of course, there's a possibility Akbar miscalculated Mr X's intentions in the chaos, but that gave him valuable time to open the garage and take his car out.' Sid is certainly a master of improvisation.

'And, in that state of chaos, rather than running back to protect his wife from this Mr X, he had the presence of mind to collect his passport, and thought it more important to close the garage door and lock it before leaving?'

'We don't know that.'

'What do you mean?' the ACP asks.

'We don't know who shut the garage door, do we?'

'We know it was closed when the police arrived at the scene. Did you close it between the time you made the call to the police and before they arrived, Mrs Khan?'

'How could I? I don't even know when the police came over. I only regained consciousness in the hospital—'

'Oh yes,' Kamala pretends she's forgotten that little fact. What is she playing at, I wonder.

'That brings me back to my question: why drug you hours before if Akbar didn't know he'd be calling Rajiv home and had no prior knowledge of Mr X coming over that evening?'

Kamala is a queen of rhetoric.

'We've covered that ground earlier—' I say.

'Yes, I know, but in light of the presence of this third, unknown man, I need to ponder again. Akbar knew Rajiv was coming over because he called him. So if Akbar was merely going to have a showdown for personal reasons why drug you? On the contrary, he'd have wanted you to see that argument so you would know that he has found out about your affair with Rajiv.'

'That's one way to interpret it.' It's Sid, sceptical, as always.

'What's the other way?' And the ACP is never short of questions.

'What I mean is that your theory – that Akbar wanted Anush to hear when he castigated Rajiv – is one way of looking at it. I think he didn't want Anush to know what he said to Rajiv that evening. Maybe he wanted to tell Rajiv to back off or risk his gravy train stopping. He might have wanted Rajiv to run away from Anush without her knowing that he had threatened Rajiv in some fashion.'

'I have to say that you've got a highly imaginative mind, Mr Dhariwal.'

'Thank you, but I'm not making this up. I'm trying to provide an alternative perspective here.'

'And I thank you for that, but in that case, Akbar could have had that conversation with Rajiv anywhere. Maybe even on the evening before when they were together, as we think. Why call him home in the evening when husband and wife are having a cosy session?'

'That beats me.'

'There's more to it, I'm sure…oh, I'm sure. I have a strong instinct I'm close, but I'm missing a few minor details in this haadsaa.' ACP

Kamala looks at me accusatorially. 'Anyway, thanks for your time, and I'll be in touch again,' she says and adds, 'soon.'

***

'It's clear she thinks you're in some way an accomplice – before or after – in the murder of Rajiv,' Aanya says. We are seated at the dining table long after the meal is over, with no incentive to move elsewhere. I don't know what the arrangements are for the night, whether Aanya will be with me or not, but that isn't relevant at this moment.

'How do you mean?' I ask.

'I think she believes you helped Akbar escape and that you know where he is now.'

'Why would I do that?'

'I know you didn't, but I get the sense she is of that opinion.'

'Besides, even if I wanted to help him, how could I have assisted Akbar in fleeing the scene after I had passed out?'

'Well, that's a very pertinent point our very own Miss Marple seems to be overlooking.'

Sid joins the dialogue.

'Oh I wish I knew where Akbar was, that he'd return tomorrow morning, and that everything would go back to normal,' I say, although I know it can never go back to how it was before. The police are looking for a murderer who, according to them, is my husband, Akbar.

'It's late. I think we should all go to bed now.'

'Another extremely pertinent point.' Sid smiles and stands up.

'I forgot to mention, I have an appointment with Dr Aryan Yadav tomorrow afternoon for the removal of my stitches. But neither of you has to tag along with me for that. I can call an Uber. It's a simple procedure and shouldn't take long,' I say.

'It's not like the Government of India will fall if I don't attend work for a day. We're not letting you go alone.'

'But—'

'No ifs or buts.'

How do I tell them that I want to be alone for a while without hurting them? They've been so nice, my saviours, in fact. Imagine facing that ACP Jha all on my own.

'Thank you,' I mouth, my eyes brimming with gratitude now, and I know if I speak I'll choke up.

'Come on, there's no reason to feel grateful or obliged. That's what friends are for.' Aanya senses my emotions. 'I'm confident that if the roles were reversed, you and Akbar would have done the same for us.'

I nod in agreement.

WEDNESDAY, 17TH JULY

Thirty-Two

Aanya drives me to the hospital after lunch. We have to wait for ten minutes before being called in. Although I booked a slot specifically with Aryan, he isn't there; he's been called into an emergency, and it is another junior doctor who removes the stitches from my forehead. I can't say whether I'm irked or relieved at not seeing him today. When I booked this appointment I had wanted to see him, but I didn't want Aanya to notice the familiarity between us. Once the media tells your entire circle of friends that you were sleeping with your husband's friend, you become conscious of these little things that you never cared about before. It's the guilt, I suppose. The doctor on duty inspects the wound and tells me that it's healing well.

'You'll have to wait a few months for the skin to settle, Mrs Khan. I doubt there will be any visible marks on your forehead. However, if there is a blemish, please don't hesitate to see a dermatologist for advice,' he says before ushering the two of us out.

'That's one less thing to worry about. Should we stop at a café on the way or do you want to go home straight, Anush?'

'I'd quite like a stop, to have some hot chocolate.'

'Great, I know a small independent café on the way; I bet you've never been to Boulangerie. They do a hot chocolate with whipped cream and marshmallows.'

'More than a thousand calories in a cup? Why not?'

'You only live once.'

And that, precisely, is the problem, I want to respond. We should have the ability to time travel, to go back and correct the bits we did wrong.

***

We decide to take an hour's nap in the afternoon when we get back before Sid returns from work. I close my eyes, and memories of the good times Akbar and I shared at the beginning of our marriage come rushing back along with tears. He was a soft-spoken, well-mannered, indisputably rich gentleman from an erstwhile royal family, who had been educated abroad. He was the jealous kind, which, initially, I was quite happy about. He had to be in love to be so protective of me, and I often revelled in that thought. As time went by, my fascination began to pale.

My father died of a heart attack, induced – as I always believed – by years of shame and indignity. Imagine his work colleagues discussing his wife in a corner or passing snide remarks. For all I know one of the many 'uncles' who visited my mother in the afternoons was his colleague. The humiliation would have been insufferable. Anyway, after his death, Akbar told me he wouldn't be accompanying me for the cremation because he didn't want to interact with '*that woman*' – my mother, he meant – so I went alone. My mother died shortly afterwards. That was my last trip to Jamnagar ever. Akbar unequivocally refused to come with me for my mother's last rites and cremation, calling her names after getting drunk. The next day he apologised, retracted his words and said that he couldn't join me on account of an important meeting he needed to attend in Delhi. But the bridge had completely burned by then. I flew to Ahmedabad and cabbed it to Jamnagar, crying all the way. Her moral compass might have been broken, but she was my mother. I knew what she did and who she was, but to hear all that from someone else, especially my husband, hurt.

That, I think, was the last straw. Our relationship never returned to what it used to be. I could never forgive the fact that he had abandoned me when I was at my lowest point. What could I expect from him? As I became distant, his jealousy started morphing into vile comments, bullying and mental abuse, sometimes physical and sexual too. That drove me to Rajiv, which in retrospect, was my biggest undoing. But I had no inkling that Rajiv was a partner in Akbar's illegal enterprise.

Correction: I hadn't the faintest notion that Akbar was involved in money laundering. A hawala shop, for heaven's sake. I could never have suspected it since I assumed he had plenty of money. I was a joint account holder in the accounts known to me, but money was never discussed in our household. However, I remember having signed hundreds of documents that Akbar brought to me for signatures. If he made me a joint holder in any of those unlawful, unauthorised accounts, would I be culpable in his criminal enterprise? I should probably check what options I have in the event that the ACP tries to drag me into something I was not even aware of.

***

'Did you say you had stitches? Where?' Sid mocks on his return. 'I can't see any blemishes, not even a scratch, Anush. You look gorgeous as ever.' He takes me in an embrace and it brings tears to my eyes. I wonder why I'm so emotional these days. 'Did the doctor say anything about what you can or cannot eat now? Or drink for that matter?'

'Nothing. He didn't even broach the subject.'

'I think,' I correct Aanya, 'that is because he had no medical history or background on how the injury had occurred or the fact that they had to flush my stomach last week to save me. For him, it was purely a clinical task – removal of stitches. If we had met one of the doctors who had been there when I was in the hospital—'

'Doctors are paid to err on the side of caution, Anush. If you're feeling fit, I think a glass of wine won't hurt.'

'If you insist.'

I barely take my first sip when the phone starts to ring.

ACP Kamala Jha.

'She simply cannot leave you alone, can she?' Aanya says.

'Here, give it to me, let me take the call.' Sid takes my phone and answers, and I can see the colour drain from his face. I can hear her talking at the other end of the phone, but she's too faint and too fast to comprehend. 'Where?' he asks. Then: 'OK, we'll be here.'

'What happened? What did she say?' Aanya beats me to it when he disconnects.

'They've tracked down Akbar's car.'

'What do you mean they've *tracked down* Akbar's car? What about Akbar?' My voice betrays my emotions. I can't imagine they've just found the car. 'What else did she say?'

'She didn't give me much, honestly; just said she'll come by in an hour.'

'Oh God.' I break down.

'There's nothing for you to worry about, Anush. The police have *tracked down the car*, it could mean nothing. We instinctively knew that had to be the case – that Akbar had to abandon the Mercedes somewhere if he wanted to disappear for the foreseeable future. It would be foolhardy to drive around in that conspicuous car if you didn't want to be found.'

'Then why did she have to call up and update us?'

'I suppose we'll know that in an hour. Let's enjoy the wine in the meantime.'

But I've lost the taste for wine. Or for anything else for that matter.

I have a choice. Everyone has that choice: to carry on or give up. However, I've decided not to play my cards, not just yet. Not until I know what cards the ACP has left to play. I won't blink first. Patience is a virtue, isn't that what they say? So I take a generous sip of wine and try to keep a calm façade. Maybe Aanya notices the slight change in my demeanour.

'Are you OK, Anush?'

'I'm fine. I'm just sick of seeing this ACP is all.' I close my eyes for a second and the memory rushes in. I can see two glasses of drinks on our coffee table in the living room, back at Sainik Farms. One filled with gin and tonic, the other with scotch. Or was it bourbon? I remember it now: Jack Daniel's. Cubes of ice. Two glasses. I picture two people drinking, I hear the ice clink, I hear *cheers* before the evening morphs into something else, and I go sideways. Each moment that arrives passes in the same instant. No matter what you do or how hard you try, you cannot suspend a particular moment in time however good or bad you feel then. The present becomes the past in a tick, leaving a memory behind that you might like or abhor. The thought brings about a myriad of emotions in me. Love. Hate. Shame. Guilt. Indeed, you cannot go back and change anything; time travel is fiction. However, the memory of what occurred in a particular moment needn't linger or be narrated as it was. It can be embellished and embroidered into a tale of your choosing.

'Maybe the ACP isn't the Miss Marple we believed she was. Maybe she's more of an acrobat in Cirque du Soleil, jumping through hoops and contorting herself to make her theories fit, just doing her part before she moves on to the next show, the next case?' Sid's voice breaks my reverie and brings a much-needed smile as I imagine ACP Kamala clumsily swinging on a rope in a leotard.

Thirty-Three

'Mrs Khan, your husband's black Mercedes E200 was captured by a camera turning left from Lado Sarai onto Sri Aurobindo Marg, towards Qutub Minar—' The ACP is back. She's standing as she pantomimes the directions with her hands, and I visualise a trapeze artist balancing herself on a tightrope – one leg of her leotard is black, one red.

'So he did drive towards Jaipur airport, as we speculated?' Sid asks while politely gesturing to ACP Jha to take a seat.

'Actually, no.'

'No?'

'No. The car was caught by the camera on Friday evening, close to midnight, almost twenty-four hours before Akbar went missing.'

'Oh, in that case, he could be there for anything. Didn't Anush tell us that he was out until late that Friday night?'

'Exactly. The car was captured turning left, and there's another camera at the point where Mehrauli–Badarpur Road merges into Sri Aurobindo Marg, but there's no sighting of Akbar's car on that one, so wherever he went, his destination must've been between these two points.'

'It's possible that he went straight towards Qutub Minar,' Sid suggests. I remain a silent spectator in the theatre of my life.

'It is possible, but he didn't. There is more than one camera surrounding the monument to ward off cavorting couples and late-night loiterers, so there is a slim chance all those devices missed his car. The car turned left from Lado Sarai and simply disappeared.'

'What do you mean disappeared?'

'It wasn't captured returning towards Sainik Farms from either of the two roads.'

'That doesn't make sense. Akbar might have taken some other route back home,' Sid argues.

'Yes, he could have, but why would he take one of the by-lanes? Who was he trying to avoid? More to the point, what caught my eye was that there was another car closely following his car that Friday night. A white Honda Civic, registration number DL1C...' ACP reads the number from the post-it she is carrying in her hand and the synapses in my brain flutter. I know that car, I've been in it. I've even made out with its owner in the back seat. 'Mrs Khan, do you know who that car belongs to?' I know that she knows the answer, but she looks me in the eye.

'Yes. Rajiv Pant.'

'So on Friday evening, the day before his murder, Rajiv followed Akbar towards Lado Sarai and they both swung a left on Sri Aurobindo Marg. Interestingly, Rajiv's car returned an hour later and was captured on the camera when the car took a left from Sri Aurobindo Marg towards Mehrauli–Badarpur Road.'

There is silence in the room for a few seconds as each one of us, I suppose, tries to visualise the route.

'It was dark, and we've enhanced the grainy black-and-white photograph from the CCTV, but it's impossible to identify the occupants—'

'Occupant-*s*?' Sid emphasises.

'I've got all the photographs enlarged and enhanced. The shots from both cars show one occupant each in the two cars when they turned left onto Aurobindo Marg but Rajiv's car, on the return journey, positively has two people in the front seats.'

'That explains it then, doesn't it?'

'That explains what, Mr Dhariwal?'

'Well, Akbar and Rajiv must have been going to the same party or wherever, and they drove up to a point in their separate cars, then for whatever reason they dropped Akbar's car at their friends' place, and carried on to their destination in Rajiv's car.'

'That is one interpretation.'

'What is the other interpretation, ACP Jha?'

'I haven't drawn any conclusions yet. My instinct tells me I'm missing something, a minor detail, a clue that can help me put all this together in a cohesive fashion. One thing that bugs me though, is that Akbar never returned to pick up his car at any time later. There are no more sightings of Rajiv's car dropping Akbar home perhaps, or of Akbar's car driving back home at any point after Friday night.'

'So maybe Rajiv dropped Akbar home.'

'What do you think, Mrs Khan?' ACP Jha squints as she glances in my direction.

'I already told you that Akbar had come home that night after I had gone to bed. I wouldn't know if someone dropped him home that night.'

'And the car?'

'I didn't see Akbar's car per se at any time between Friday and Saturday, I already told you. It was only fair to assume, at the time, that if Akbar was home, his car would be outside. I didn't ask, he didn't mention it.'

'Isn't this just a case of repetition, ACP Jha? We seem to be going over the same events again.'

'No, Mr Dhariwal, don't you see this latest discovery changes everything?'

'How so?'

'If Akbar didn't have his car at home on Saturday, how did he flee after the murder? Either he escaped on foot, which means he couldn't have gone too far…or someone gave him a lift.'

'Which brings us back to the possibility of a third person present at the scene that night, besides Akbar and Rajiv.'

'And…that also highlights that Akbar's car might still be where he parked it on Friday night, a day before Rajiv's murder since we know he wasn't driven back to the same place, not by Rajiv, at least…'

'For all we know Akbar might have called Rajiv that Saturday evening to drive him back to the venue to pick up his car, that's all. And something entirely different, rather sinister, awaited both of them when Rajiv arrived,' Sid adds.

'Well, all that is hypothetical. We might be adding pieces that don't belong to this puzzle at all, Mr Dhariwal. All we have are speculations and opinions. Guesswork. There is little evidence to support any of this, don't you think?'

'Honestly, I don't know what to think. I'm trying to help. Sometimes, if you speculate on the circumstances or sequence of events, I'd like to believe it may give you a clue to look for evidence in the precise place.'

'I get that,' the ACP nods. 'So…if we were to go with the course of events you hypothesise, Mr Dhariwal, Akbar's car should still be parked somewhere between the two points the CCTVs lost it, which is a distance of merely what, a kilometre or a bit more. And maybe, Akbar is there too.'

'Akbar doesn't know anyone living there,' I tell her.

'And you know that how, Mrs Khan?' I realise the ACP has not once called me by my given name. She's always referred to me as Mrs Khan while she calls Akbar and Rajiv by their first names. She is keeping it formal. Is there a reason? Should I be worried?

'I'm his wife,' I say confidently.

'That is hardly a bulletproof reason, no pun intended. And pardon my impertinence, but from what I've gathered speaking with you, you didn't know a lot about your husband.' I look at her as though someone has slapped me across the face, in public no less.

'Like I said, pardon my incivility,' she continues poker-faced. 'But it was *you* who told me that you never suspected your husband was running a hawala shop. *You* said you had no inkling he had benami bank accounts held under diverse names or the amount of money those accounts held.'

I nod. I can't contest that.

'Didn't you say that your husband told you he'd be late on Friday night because he was dining with customers from abroad? But as it turns out there were no visitors that day – the staff at the office confirmed that. You don't even know what time Akbar returned home and got into the same bed as you that evening or whether he drove back in his car or was dropped home by Rajiv or someone else. You don't know who tried to throttle you from behind, who bashed your head against the mirror in your house, who banged at your bedroom door when you called the police…you want me to carry on? Forgive me for stating all this but you don't give me much confidence when you suggest: *I-am-his-wife-so-I-know-everything*, because you're arguing against yourself.'

The bitch has a sardonic smile on her face.

Another slap across my face. I shut up. Sid senses my humiliation and takes over the conversation immediately.

'You're correct, ACP Jha. It just might be that Akbar is still in that area, and if we look—'

'Thanks for the heads-up, Mr Dhariwal. The thought never crossed my mind.' She's being sarcastic with Sid too. 'Believe me, my teams are going door-to-door, searching every single building within a one-kilometre radius as we speak. Like I keep telling you, I'm missing just a—'

'Minor detail, we know,' Sid completes.

'Now, if you'll excuse me, I think I'll be working through the night to find that proverbial needle. Have a good evening.'

***

'What minor detail does she keep referring to?' Aanya sounds annoyed.

'Only two people know what that is.' Sid has been savouring his wine the whole time the ACP was here, talking to us. Aanya and I had stopped after our first servings. I have a feeling ACP Jha wouldn't have been so uptight and surly if Sid had poured her a glass too. I remember he had offered and she, being on duty, had declined.

'Two people?' I hear Aanya ask. I don't even want to go there. I want that door to shut forever, this inquiry to conclude, and my life to return to whatever the new normal is; I want to move on. The earlier this is over, the quicker I can go back home.'

'Of course, there are two of them. ACP Kamala Jha and God almighty.' Sid chuckles. 'You girls sure you don't want any more wine?'

'No, and I think you should stop after this one too. I'm calling for dinner to be served.'

'Jo hukum mere aaqa. I'll just step out for a smoke.'

'I didn't know you smoked.' I know I have no business asking. I'm not his wife, I'm not his mother.

'I sometimes do when I'm stressed.'

Aanya rolls her eyes and walks out to the kitchen.

'What are you stressed about?'

'All this police business is stressful, Anush.'

'But she's only here because of me. If I move into a hotel—'

'Don't say that. We are in this together, Anush.'

Has he inadvertently poked a beehive or does he know something he's not telling me? I wonder. *How much can I trust him? And Aanya?*

THURSDAY, 18TH JULY

Thirty-Four

'Piyush and I have been worried sick about you, babe. Is everything all right?' Monica calls after breakfast. She wants me to come over again this weekend, but I'm in no mental disposition to spend any more time with them. What's the point of merely having me over for the weekend anyway? For one, this repeated, periodic moving between friends' homes makes me feel like a nomad, and cognitively reiterates that I'm homeless at present, which makes me even more miserable than I already am, if that's even possible. Secondly, I remember that my experience at Monica and Piyush's place last time around wasn't terribly joyful. On the contrary, I disliked Piyush's lopsided comments and insinuations, and his total disrespect for how much Sid was doing for me. I find Sid and Aanya extremely supportive, especially Sid – the way he takes over the conversations with ACP Jha, and how he puts forth other possibilities or argues his point like a lawyer fighting my corner in court. For everything new the ACP comes up with, he has, as yet, always found a viable alternative theory, and as it happens, the ACP hasn't been able to find a fracture in his postulations.

'I'd love to be with you both, but I think Aanya's planned something this weekend, so I'll have to excuse myself, Monica,' I explain mclancholically.

'It's just that we told Mira that you might be over, and asked her to cancel a birthday party she had been invited to...'

I wonder if Mira's chemistry problems have been sorted at school. Mira is unquestionably a lovely girl, and quite affectionate. But she's fourteen. In the last year, every time I've met her, she's shown no interest in any of her parents' friends. She's always on her phone chatting with boys or with her other friends about boys. I have a feeling she's been detained at home for some misconduct;

the corollary being that I'll have a grumpy teenager along with her unpleasant dad to deal with. My answer is no.

'Do you want me to speak to Aanya?'

'Of course not,' I say affirmatively; then I realise that I've said it a bit too quickly but so be it. I've had enough of other people making decisions on my behalf. I've decided to stay put.

'What about next weekend – I can ask Mira to stay back to see you?'

'I'm sorry, but I'll have to let you know about it next week.'

'How is the police inquiry coming along? Are they any closer to finding Akbar?'

'The policewoman has been here to see me a few times, but I doubt she's closing in,' I respond. I see no reason to tell Monica the minutiae of the investigation, to keep her updated.

'Please don't hesitate to call me or Piyush if you need any help, babe.'

'Of course, thank you, Monica.'

'And take care of yourself, babe.'

***

I see no merit in telling Aanya that I've declined a weekend with Monica and Piyush. I wonder what she'd think if she came to know that they're stuck with me for longer than they initially anticipated. I have, to my credit, asked my hosts if I should move into a hotel, and they've vehemently protested, so I know I'm not stepping on their toes. Not yet at any rate. I need to ask the ACP how long it will be before I can go home, and if the investigation is going to take longer than another week, I might book a hotel and inform Aanya later. I can't be overstaying my welcome here. These two are the only real friends I have left.

'What's the plan?' Aanya asks me as we have coffee in the garden early next morning. Sid hasn't joined us; I believe he's getting ready for work, which means Aanya is taking another day off work for me.

'If the ACP doesn't drop by again with another tangential discovery, you mean?' I smile.

'She is *something*. I can't read her. At times, she's OK, but other times she's completely obnoxious and accusatory. But let's go out today, maybe for brunch. It'll be good to get out. We won't go far so if she calls, we can always return within an hour. She can't just barge in without calling you first. In any event, I think she should come around when Sid is present. What do you think?'

'Absolutely. I am glad Sid and you have taken it upon yourselves to help me through this crisis,' I say, tears forming in my eyes.

'We're always there for you and Akbar, although we don't know when we'll see Akbar next. By the way, Sid has spoken to one of the best lawyers in Delhi, and he's on call the moment we find Akbar. I hope he comes to us before the police get to him. It would be best if Akbar and this lawyer – I can't recollect the name Sid told me – go into the police station to surrender after bail or some kind of legal settlement has already been arranged—'

'Bail?' I almost cry out.

'Anush, neither of us knows what exactly happened that night, but the police are looking for Akbar in connection with Rajiv's homicide…so we don't care how and why the ACP is sugar-coating it for us, but there is bound to be an arrest warrant out for him, no questions about that. The lawyer advised Sid that if Akbar presents himself along with the lawyer at a police station it will be a lot better than the police arresting him. Surrendering will go a long way in helping Akbar later when the case goes to court, which appears inevitable considering the circumstances.'

'Oh?'

'We need to be prepared is all.'

'Yes.' I realise I'm actually choking.

'You're not convinced?'

'I am. I just can't tell you how indebted I feel…' I burst into tears. I can't believe they've taken all this trouble without mentioning anything to me.

'Shut up, Anush. This is the least we can do.'

'Thanks,' I almost whisper.

'Also, it's better to engage a lawyer now. We need some ammunition should the police play dirty—'

'You think ACP Jha is bent?'

'No, but it won't be the first time a piece of evidence has been planted or lost. You see what I mean?'

I don't, but I nod my head. I hope it won't come to that.

'Let's go to a spa, we need some pampering.'

***

'Any news from our ACP sahiba?' Sid asks on his return from work in the evening. Aanya and I had spent the day at a local spa. I hadn't realised how much I needed the break until I got there. 'It's been almost twenty-four hours since we last heard from ACP Jha. I don't know what to make of that.'

'Maybe she's found Akbar's car,' Aanya says.

'Or Akbar?'

But we hear nothing from her the entire evening. We contemplate calling her and asking for an update but decide otherwise. If she's busy why pull her out of the investigation? The consensus is that if she had discovered something, she'd have called us. Or perhaps dropped by without an appointment.

'Let's wait until tomorrow. I'll call her in the morning to ask,' Sid tells us.

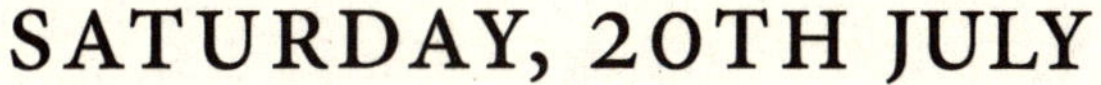

SATURDAY, 20TH JULY

Thirty-Five

Nothing of consequence happened yesterday. It was the first day since the haadsaa that went by without a visit from Kumari Kamala, and thank God for that. She has become a pain. I wish she just went away. However, the day got better when someone from the Saket Police Station called and told me that the police had completed their search and investigation, and our Sainik Farms residence would be opened for me to return to later in the evening. I couldn't have been happier. I love being with Sid and Aanya, but I have already taxed them enough. Moreover, being in your own home is always another level of comfort. You can do what you like when you like. You can wake up when you want and wear pyjamas the entire day. Given the circumstances, I feel I am about to buckle under the pressure of my friends' compassion and pity, which is genuine in their case, and yet it inundates me with guilt.

***

This morning, I wake up to a sliver of sunlight and its warmth finding its way through the slits between the curtains. It's still early and I cannot hear any other sounds. I look at my iPhone and it's only 6.35 a.m. I know it will be impossible to sleep any more. Closing my eyes reminds me of the pivotal Saturday night two weeks ago. The drinks. The drugs. The smashed mirror. The gunshot. My mind struggles to process, to accept. If I think too hard, I might have a breakdown, and going back to the hospital is the last thing I want. Try as hard as I might, not a single pleasant memory surfaces. Not one.

I decide to get up and make a coffee for myself. It's the weekend, and Sid and Aanya had gone out for dinner at someone's place last evening. I had declined to join them although they asked me to join. I am in no mental frame to meet other people who may or may not know me but still recognise me; I was in no mood to answer any questions about Akbar, about the murder, about Rajiv, about anything.

As the coffee brews, I wonder where ACP Jha is. Sid called her yesterday morning and left a message, but she did not return his call. We haven't heard from her since Wednesday evening when she visited us here. Where is she? What has she discovered now that she isn't telling us? Anything more suspicious or nothing at all? Don't they say nothing suspicious is highly suspicious or something to that effect? Her silence is certainly not helping to put my mind at rest.

Aanya walks into the kitchen in her satin shorts and nightshirt, looking gorgeous even with her messy hair. 'I thought I heard you, good morning.'

'Did I wake you up?'

'Nah, I was up, just being lazy, wasting time on social media.'

Damn! I haven't looked at social media at all in two weeks now. I wonder what stories are being propagated by friends and friends of friends. In these times, the true representation of what people think appears in their posts and comments on social platforms, sometimes directly, sometimes indirectly. With the media having blown the lid off my affair with my husband's friend, his murder and my husband taking off, it must be enough fodder to last a few months.

'Black, no sugar?' I pour coffee for both of us.

'Yes.'

'Anything about me or Akbar on social?'

'My recommendation would be to avoid logging in for a few more weeks.'

'So a lot, then?'

She takes a sip of the hot brew and nods.

'Hmm…'

'And let me warn you that people's opinions vary from—'

'Me being a whore to a battered wife?'

'You got it, and neither avatar is pretty to read about.'

'Good morning, ladies.' Sid walks in and, luckily, there is some extra coffee for him, too. He loves full-fat milk and two spoons of sugar. 'I have an early morning text from our very own Miss Marple: she's on her way here in an hour.'

'Did she say what about?'

'Well, she didn't say. I tried calling her back when I read the text, but it went straight to her voicemail, so either she's out of reach or she doesn't want to talk on the phone.'

'Probably the latter,' Aanya murmurs, rolls her eyes and finishes her coffee.

Sid takes his coffee and, sensing we are in the middle of a conversation, walks away.

'Anyone in particular?' I am hesitant to look at the posts from various friends, as I can envisage the sort of comments and the language used to express them, but I can't resist knowing if someone has been exceptionally vitriolic.

'Your friend, Sonya.'

'She's not my friend.' I remember the woman very well. Twice divorced, always scarce of clothes at all parties, an incorrigible coquette with a reputation. Rumour has it that she has no buttons or zippers to hold her skirts in place. I distinctly recall her flagrant flirting with Akbar on more than a few occasions. She almost disregarded the fact that I was present and watching her. That's her game. Throwing a gauntlet to the wives or girlfriends present. It's more of an ego trip for her than anything else. The fact that she's stunning and single somehow shifts the brains of some men from their craniums to between their legs. She's shameless. And it peeves me that someone who proclaims to be open-minded has a word or two to say about me.

'And I don't want to prejudice your opinion, but our friend Monica – although she hasn't posted anything or commented on any of those posts – has liked some of Sonya's and other people's comments on them. Just so you know. I mean if you log in you can see for yourself, but since you asked, I thought I should make you aware that people aren't what they say or what they want you to believe.'

I am more than peeved now. I feel enraged. 'And she had the gall to call me earlier this week to ask if I wanted to come over to their house this weekend?'

'Really? You never told me.'

'I declined, as I wasn't comfortable the last time around. Anyway, let me go for a shower if we have to be ready before bloody Kamala arrives.'

Thirty-Six

'Could I move back into my home today?' I am frustrated by repeated visits from ACP Jha and her questioning while giving nothing in return.

'We shall come to that, Mrs Khan, but we have a lot to discuss today.' She has that sly smile again. Like a cat that has found a bowl of cream.

'Have you found Akbar's car?' Sid asks.

'Yes, and a lot more, Mr Dhariwal, but I have a request. I'd ideally like to speak to Mrs Khan alone, but I know that isn't possible. For one, I can see she still hasn't recovered completely from her shock, and secondly, if I try to block you out, you'll go over my head and get a sign-off from my boss, which I'm aware of. So—'

'Is Anush a suspect?'

'No. If she were, I'd be asking her questions at the police station, not in your living room. Now, if I may, please?'

'Sure, go ahead.' I spare Sid the ignominy of responding.

'Do you know if Rajiv Pant owned or rented a garage in the weeks preceding his death?'

'No.'

'So you weren't aware of it at all?'

'No.'

'Mrs Khan, if you do, please don't lie as it will imminently come out, so I urge you to think carefully if he ever mentioned it in a conversation to you or in passing or if you saw any paperwork when you visited him at his apartment?'

'No. I don't know about the existence of any other property rented or owned by Rajiv except the Gurgaon apartment he resided in.'

'Hmm…' she responds. 'The garage is located off the one-kilometre stretch on Sri Aurobindo Marg between Lado Sarai and Mahrauli–Badarpur Road junctions. Exactly where Akbar's car was spotted late Friday night before disappearing, never to be seen again.'

'So you found the car then?' Sid jumps in.

'Mr Dhariwal, I have politely asked you to refrain from intervening, but if you can't then I'll have to ask you to leave the room. Please.' ACP Jha might have kept her tone polite, but there is no civility in the words.

Sid merely nods.

'The said garage is on an acre of gated, barren land with a boundary wall, about half a kilometre from the main road. It was rented two weeks ago by Mr Rajiv Pant. An amount of four lakh sixty thousand rupees as rent for the entire year was paid in advance. Would you know why Rajiv Pant would need to hire a secluded property like that, Mrs Khan?'

'My guess is as good as yours, ACP Jha. I told you I didn't even know he had rented this place.'

'Well, I believe you when you say you didn't know about it until something comes up that tells me otherwise. However, you are a smart woman, Mrs Khan, so if you were to speculate what would you say was the intended purpose of this isolated piece of land with a garage?'

'I have no idea whatsoever. I mean, I wasn't aware of a lot of what transpired between Akbar and Rajiv—'

'Let's leave Akbar out of it for the time being, please. We shall come back to him in a minute.'

'OK, as long as you know that my biggest worry is Akbar at the moment, not Rajiv or a piece of land he rented or the purpose he bought or rented it for.'

'I am very aware of that, Mrs Khan.'

'Thank you,' I respond sarcastically, although anyone can see that I'm shaking with fear, but I don't want to exhibit my dread to the ACP. 'So you found Akbar's car at this place?'

'Mrs Khan, I am not responding to your questions until I get answers to all of mine. Are we clear?'

Damn you! 'Yes.'

'But to assuage your anxiety, yes, we found a black Mercedes model E200 – just like your husband's – on this piece of land I mentioned. The registration plates weren't on the car and the experts are verifying using the Vehicle Identification Number if it's the same car. The likelihood is that it's the same vehicle, but until the VIN matches the records, technically I cannot confirm that it is Akbar's car.'

'And Akbar?'

'No more questions, please.'

'OK,' I resign.

'Whoever left that car there must have left it on the Friday night before Rajiv's murder since we saw it being driven there on camera... before we saw Rajiv leave from the other road with a passenger in the front seat. But I've already told you about all this before.'

I merely nod. She's repeating her questions and giving us theories to see if we react, to check if there is something we know that we aren't telling her. I've already lied to her, at least by omission. Maybe she knows, and she's only playing me. I need to be careful and alert.

'Coffee, I need a coffee. What about you, ACP Jha?'

If she knows that I'm dallying, she doesn't show it. Her poker face is one of her strongest assets.

'I'll have one too, why not?'

I get up with Aanya and go into the kitchen. I need to compose myself.

***

'So this place in the wilderness – for lack of a better, more appropriate word – that Rajiv Pant rented, does it still puzzle you or have you come up with any plausible explanation, however weird, as to why he rented it, Mrs Khan?'

She knows something, this bitch. Despite my saying I didn't know anything about it, she knows something. Or is it a mere suspicion? Why did I have to lie? I could have said yes; I didn't have to know where this place was and for what purpose. But here we are. One inane lie might now require a hundred damaging ones to cover up. But if she's found the garage and the car, then…nevertheless, I shouldn't assume the outcome.

'No idea?' She breaks my unnecessary musing.

'None,' I maintain. I remain standing while she sits and sips her coffee.

'Let's move on then, Mrs Khan. Do you remember, I had asked you about a big freezer Rajiv had purchased days before his death?'

I nod.

'And the seller who sold this freezer confirmed that it was delivered to your house in Sainik Farms, remember?'

'And I'm equally certain that no such freezer was ever delivered to our place.'

'Of course not. We found the freezer along with Akbar's car in the same garage on Rajiv's property. We've checked the serial numbers and it's the same piece. Do you want to know what else we found in that locked garage, Mrs Khan?'

'What?'

'Your husband, Akbar Khan—'

'You found Akbar and you're telling me now?' I scream at her.

'We didn't find Akbar Khan alive. We found his corpse inside that freezer.'

My knees buckle, and I almost fall to the ground. Thankfully, Sid is nearby and catches me before I hit the floor. I hear Kamala tell Sid that the police have to return to our Sainik Farms property again this morning to carry out a fresh search.

Of all the thoughts that can cross my mind, it's my mother's words that come to the forefront: 'Always remember, Anush, life is like a game of Snakes and Ladders; the snake bites to bring you down, the ladder helps you rise. And unless you cheat by tampering with the dice it's a game of pure luck. No matter how far ahead you are, one snakebite is all that's needed to level the game. But that can work in your favour too. So it is never over until it's over...' Akbar's corpse certainly feels like a snakebite at this point.

Thirty-Seven

When I open my eyes, I'm in bed. I'm in the Dhariwals' guest room again; the curtains are drawn, but I can sense that night has descended. I remember losing it when ACP Jha told me about finding Akbar's corpse. What happened next? I sit up rather quickly and my head spins.

Perhaps Aanya gave me a sedative, but I have no memory of it. Did I pass out in the living room? Is the ACP still around waiting for me to wake up? I try again slowly and go to the bathroom, wash my face and walk to the living room. Aanya and Sid are alone, having a drink.

'What happened to me?'

'You needed a little rest, Anush.'

'What time is it?'

'Past nine in the evening.'

'Where is ACP Jha?'

'She wanted us to wake you up, but we told her off. She's gone for now but she'll be back tomorrow morning.'

'Where is Akbar?'

'He's...he's no more, I'm so sorry, Anush.' Aanya steps forward and takes me in her arms. Our heads on each other's shoulders, the tears flow freely.

'We truly are.' Sid joins us and puts his arms around both of us. 'I never imagined something like this could happen to Akbar even though I was the one who had theorised that there was someone else – Mr X – along with Rajiv at your door the other day.'

I break down. I can see that Aanya is equally distraught.

'The police need to focus on finding this third, as yet unidentified, man as soon as possible. He is at the heart of all this. I've called up my contacts to exert pressure on ACP Jha. She's been barking up the wrong tree, trying to be an over-achiever by asking irrelevant questions to ascertain if we knew about Rajiv hiring a place, buying a freezer…for fuck's sake.' Sid's temper rises with every sentence.

'Akbar…' I cry out.

'Akbar chased the wrong guy or tried to escape when he saw Mr X shooting Rajiv. Whatever the case may be, he ended up in that freezer. Oh God…!' Even Sid isn't immune to the tears. 'No one knows what happened that night, Anush. Rajiv might have been preparing for something, but it did not end well.'

'Are you saying Rajiv was planning to murder someone and put him in the freezer?' Aanya asks.

'I don't know. He never came across as strong to me – to kill someone and dispose of the body in this manner needs metal balls, and I don't think Rajiv had them, unless someone helped him or forced him to. To think that he was planning to kill Akbar is out of the question, whatever the differences they might have had between them.'

Sid thankfully doesn't say that the differences were spawned because I slept with Rajiv.

'In any event, Rajiv couldn't have killed Akbar since he ended up dead himself. Even a moron can see that they couldn't have killed each other if their bodies were found in different places.'

'Poor you.' Aanya tries to console me. My phone begins to ring.

'I'll get it,' Sid says as he goes to retrieve my phone from the guest room. A sixth sense tells me that this call is ominous, and I'm not wrong.

'We'll be there in the morning.'

'That bloody Kamala again?' Aanya asks.

'You're correct.'

'What does she want now?'

'She wants Anush to come in to identify Akbar, since she's the next of kin. Then she wants Anush to meet her at Sainik Farms. She says she has to show her something there.'

'We're going with you, Anush,' Aanya states matter-of-factly.

'Of course we are, there was never a doubt in my mind.'

I wish they wouldn't, but I don't have any strength left to argue. 'Could I have a stiff drink please?' I ask Sid.

SUNDAY, 21ST JULY

Thirty-Eight

Akbar tells me how gorgeous I am. He says he can't stay away from me for a single day. He slowly removes my clothes and steps back to look at me. He says I am an angel visiting this earth solely for him. He makes love to me passionately. He murmurs that he loves me, that he will love me until eternity and beyond, that he'll never let anyone or anything come between us. If anyone ever tried, God help them. He's mildly possessive, but his true colours would only surface later. I love Akbar, too, but as time progresses, I start to dread him, and then loathe him. His lovemaking gets rougher over time; it feels like he punishes me for things he dislikes. He likes to see me in tight-fitting outfits, but he doesn't want anyone else to see me in them.

I wake up confused. What I saw was a dream or a nightmare. I can't even say if it wasn't something I imagined while I was semi-conscious. My life has been spiralling down for quite some time now, not just these past two weeks. What happened two weeks back was a culmination of it all; it wasn't great before that either, but it wasn't so terrible.

***

The AIIMS – All India Institute of Medical Sciences – is where the police took Akbar. Or rather, his body. Sid told me that he had found out, through his political connections, that the autopsy had taken a lot longer than expected given that Akbar's body was frozen, having been found in a freezer. Another consequence of the body being frozen was that the forensic pathologist could not establish the precise time of death.

'I studied a bit of science back in college. I know that there is no body of knowledge available to humans to accurately determine the time of death unless someone sees it happening. It is largely based on factors like the cooling of the body if it's kept at room temperature, and even in that event, the best pathologists can only provide a window that is an hour or two within which they assess that someone must have died. Never the exact time,' Sid explains as we drive to AIIMS. 'Unfortunately, in Akbar's case, it is impossible to even determine the exact day. Did he pass away on Saturday, the night Rajiv was shot or the day after or possibly even later?'

'Let's not talk about all this, please,' Aanya tells him off.

ACP Jha isn't around. She has left one of her uniformed officers to take care of the formalities here. Akbar wasn't decapitated or disfigured in any way. Anyone who has seen his photograph could recognise and identify him. It's routine practice that the police ask a relative or someone close to identify the body in such cases. The clinician present explains that Akbar died of asphyxiation. *He was smothered,* are his words. He explains that he's concluded that Akbar wasn't garrotted based on the fact that there were no ligature marks on the neck whatsoever.

'What I find most peculiar is that there were no other injuries on his body which meant that he didn't fight his assailant either,' he adds, as he gestures to us towards a room that is as cold as a freezer. The irony isn't lost on me – Akbar's body was thawed to perform the autopsy only to be sewn up later and put into this room.

I know what I came here for. I've heard the clinician talk about Akbar in great detail and yet I fall down when I see Akbar, cold on a gurney. It will remain one of the most harrowing experiences of my life, I know. Identifying someone's body, someone you once loved, can only look painless in films. My knees give way. It takes both Sid and Aanya to pull me up.

Then, there are other procedures to follow, forms to sign.

'Strange, isn't it?' Sid asks. 'Akbar was a strong man. Why wouldn't he have fought back?'

'That's not for me to comment on, sir.'

***

We arrive at Sainik Farms at around three-fifteen in the afternoon. The sun is bright. Our garden still has some flowers left. Unlike my last visit, there aren't four uniformed police officers outside. But when we go in, there are two officers accompanying ACP Jha. So my home was out of police possession for less than sixteen hours since that fateful night.

'Good afternoon.' She is such a serpent; she says it buoyantly, as if we've come here for a celebration. It is time for dread when the snake attempts to charm you, isn't it?

I nod in response. Does she expect me to be cheerful when I've come here directly after identifying my husband's body?

'I've been informed by my team that the proceedings went smoothly.'

'It took hours,' Sid complains.

'Well, such things involve both the medical team and the police; twice the bureaucracy, double the work. I'm sorry.' Her tone is hardly apologetic; neither is her body language.

'What is it that you need from us?' Sid asks.

'Nothing from you two, to be honest. I just want to have a chat with Mrs Khan, iron out some finer details, that's it.' She stares Sid in the eye, challenging him to an argument. He is smart enough not to take the bait.

'But we can stay around, yes?'

'As long as Mrs Khan is OK with you being present, I have no objections.'

Sid looks at me, and I give him a slight nod. I want them to stay. More to the point, I don't want to be left alone with this vile woman and the two police constables.

'But I request both of you to refrain from interjecting, however strongly you might feel the urge to say something, please. Save your observations and questions, and we can talk about them later.'

Sid and Aanya look at each other, then nod.

'Shall we...?' ACP Kamala gestures towards the living room.

To an outsider watching us, it would seem as if this is her house and I am the guest. I am beginning to detest her now. We follow her into the living room and sit on the sofas.

'Unfortunately, I am not the host, and consequently, I can't offer you anything from the kitchen, but if you want, I can send one of the constables to get a drink from one of the nearby shops.'

'Some chilled drinks would be good,' Sid requests.

'There should be some in the refrigerator.' I point towards the kitchen.

'Are you sure?' the ACP asks. Sid gets up to go, but she stops him. 'Mr Dhariwal, it's best if one of my constables fetches them, please.'

What is this? I want to ask. The police have been in my house for two weeks. What evidence can Sid or I or anyone possibly pinch or contaminate now?

'When are you planning to vacate the property this time?' I ask instead.

'Soon, very soon, Mrs Khan.'

'But if you released it last evening, what prompted you to return for a fresh search?'

'Sorry to put it inconsiderately, but last week your husband was missing, and this week your husband's corpse has been found. That changes things for us.'

'How?'

'Last week he was a murder suspect, now he's another victim. With that in mind, we need to go through the house all over again.'

I start to cry.

The constable brings cans of diet cola and cartons of orange juice. He doesn't bother with glasses.

'What do you want to know that I haven't already told you?' I ask after taking a few sips of diet cola.

'Some of it might be repetitive, Mrs Khan, so please bear with me. I need to be thorough so that I don't miss or ignore or misinterpret anything.'

I nod my acquiescence.

She picks up a large notebook from the table by her side, which I hadn't noticed earlier. 'So going back to the Friday night—'

'You mean the night before Rajiv…?'

'Died? Yes, and excuse me since I will need to refer to my notes from time to time to confirm. In your statement, you said you were alone in the house after the servants left around…what time did you say the last person left?'

'I don't remember you asking me or me telling you the time, but it must have been around six-fifteen.'

'And you remember the time when the last person left, how?'

'I don't remember the exact time, but that's when they usually leave on Fridays if Akbar and I are weekending alone.'

'Noted.' She makes a note. Of what, I don't know. I think she's being theatrical, but I can't say.

'And, according to your previous statement, Akbar came home around…?'

I know what she's doing. She's going over and over the same questions to see if there's a hole in my narrative. Does she think I'm still on drugs?

'As far as I remember, I very explicitly told you that I don't know what time Akbar returned that Friday evening. I had already gone to bed before he returned. The next time I saw him was on Saturday morning.'

'Do you drink alcohol, Mrs Khan?'

'What kind of a question is that?' I ask tersely. 'You know I do. I told the doctors and you that Akbar and I were having drinks when Rajiv came by that night.'

'Oh yes, I'm sorry. I meant, do you drink a lot?'

'Describe a lot, please?' It seems like the discussion Sid and I had the other night.

'Do you drink daily?'

'No.'

'Did you drink on the Friday night in question?'

'I might've had a glass of wine or two, but I was in my senses, if that's what you're asking.'

'OK, we take it that you have no clue what time Akbar returned home that night. In that case, I guess it is redundant to ask if you heard a car drop him home, correct?'

'Yes, correct.'

'Or just hypothetically speaking, if no car came into your driveway that night you wouldn't have known – am I correct?'

'How do you mean?'

'You didn't hear anything since you were asleep, so perhaps Akbar didn't come home that Friday night?'

'Then he must've come in the morning.'

'So you say, but no one saw him in the morning either. Or at any time after that.'

'How can you say that? He made coffee for me, we had a meal together—'

'I meant no one except you, Mrs Khan. No one except you saw Akbar or his car after Friday night.'

A chill runs down my spine.

Thirty-Nine

'What are you insinuating, ACP Jha?' Despite being warned by her, Sid speaks up.

'It's one of our working theories, Mr Dhariwal,' she responds, still looking at me. 'Mrs Khan says she drank a glass of wine or two, but maybe she had more than that, and she didn't see Akbar but, maybe, imagined him since that's what *should* have been. What if she had been put on mild drugs on Friday itself, and she doesn't remember the chronology of events as lucidly as she might think?'

'What nonsense!' I cry out.

'I'm sorry, Mrs Khan, but you have to appreciate that I'm taking you into confidence by running these theories past you. Usually, the police don't do that.'

Should I be obliged? I'm fuming.

'Moving on,' she says before I can put in a defence that I wasn't out of my senses on Friday night or Saturday morning. 'While you were awake, you said you were watching television and surfing channels.'

'Yes.'

'Did someone visit you?'

'No.' She's asked me all this before.

'Can you remember what you were watching that night?'

'I think I watched some of the highlights of the IPL match that had been played earlier in the day before squandering time surfing the channels to find something else to watch after the highlights were over.'

'What match was it, do you remember?'

This woman is being thorough. And irritating. But I know my stuff.

'It was Rajasthan Royals versus Delhi Capitals.'

'I love Shikhar Dhawan.'

What is this? Sorority girls drooling over cricketers now?

'He's brilliant. He scored fifty runs that day and took the team to victory.' I am guessing she wants to establish if I was really in front of the television. This should satisfy her curiosity, but no…

'Surprising, isn't it? The last time I asked you this question you couldn't even recollect what you were watching, and if I'm correct you mentioned you were watching something on Netflix… and now you even know that Dhawan scored a fifty.' Her tone is definitely sarcastic.

'I hope you haven't forgotten, ACP Jha, that the last time you asked me questions, I had just come out of the hospital – where I had been admitted due to trauma and overdose, so my mind wasn't as sharp as it is now,' I respond sardonically. Tit for tat and all that, but I know she's in a position of advantage. I should be mindful of my approach.

'Oh yes, yes, yes, true! There are so many things going on in my mind. I'm sorry, no offence.'

'None taken.'

'Good, so no one visited you on Friday evening…' the ACP is murmuring and conspicuously striking something in her notebook. Histrionics. Is anything even written on those pages?

'What are you thinking?' Sid can't stop himself.

Either ACP Jha doesn't care any more or she is distracted or maybe she's through with me so she responds to him directly. 'You remember I told you Akbar's car was spotted on CCTV on Friday night, but never captured anywhere after that?'

'Yes.'

'We thought something untoward might've occurred on Friday night, but Mrs Khan is confident that no one visited her on Friday evening, and then asserts waking up to coffee prepared by Akbar on Saturday morning. There goes one of my theories out of the window.'

'But that doesn't make sense. Akbar drove to that secluded piece of land that we now know belonged to Rajiv, left his car and drove here with Rajiv after wherever they went that evening.'

'That is what our initial premise was, but I don't think it's as simple as that. Something's missing.'

'Do you think that's not what happened? You said there were two people in the car while returning?'

'I did, but we don't know who that second person is, do we?'

***

'Mrs Khan, when Akbar – or this third man, as yet unidentified, who Mr Dhariwal has referred to as Mr X – pushed you against the mirror in your entrance hall, you fell down, didn't you?' The ACP resembles a dog that's discovered an elephant's femur, which she has been gnawing at for over two hours now. My mind has gone completely numb, and I haven't the faintest idea what she's trying to imply.

'Yes.'

'Did you not look behind at all to see who had pushed you?'

'No. It happened so suddenly. Someone seized me by the neck from behind and forced my head against the mirror. I was utterly shocked, as you can imagine. I was not in a state to look back and take in who it was.'

'And you rushed to your bedroom and secured the door from the inside…' She reads from her notes. 'Yes, you mentioned that to me.'

'Thank you.'

'And you heard the gunshot from your bedroom.'

'Yes.'

'Did someone – Akbar or Rajiv or Mr X or anyone else – enter the bedroom after the gunshot?'

'No.'

'Hmm…Constable Bhim Singh,' she calls out. 'Bring *that*, please.'

The three of us look at each other. What is *that*?

I see the big-shouldered, moustachioed Bhim Singh walking towards us with a clear plastic bag – the sort they present as evidence in television series – containing tan leather gloves.

I know where this conniving policewoman is headed; oh, I do! Does she think I am unripe fruit that fell from the tree last night? I may not have passed the bar, but I have studied the law enough to skirt around it. I've had two weeks to think. Admittedly, for the first few days, I was groggy and under the influence of all the medication, but I still had plenty of time to dwell on this.

I should have known that the choices I made would have consequences, and certainly not the ones I had anticipated in this event. Most certainly not. Not all stories have a happy ending, do they? Blood rushes through my veins, flooding my brain and giving me an intense headache; a wave of nausea makes my head spin, my body turns hot like a coal pit and itches with anxiety. Morbid anxiety.

'Is everything OK, Mrs Khan?' the policewoman asks. She's such a bitch.

'Yeah.'

Bhim Singh places the packet containing gloves between us on the coffee table. Aanya and Sid glance at the packet, then at me. I wonder what they might be thinking. Does it matter?

'Do you recognise these gloves, Mrs Khan?'

I nod.

Given the circumstances, the faint-hearted and the feeble-minded may envision their lives crumbling in that instant, but not me. I refuse to allow that to happen.

I remember my mother's parallelism with life. Snakes and Ladders. Pick up a game board of Snakes and Ladders from any manufacturer around the globe, and you will find that they all share one common feature: there is always a snake lurking between ninety-five and a hundred to bring you down. I'm on ninety-five, and this ACP is on ninety-eight. The game, as they say, is afoot.

'I take it as a yes.'

'Yes.'

'Are they yours?'

'No.'

'Would you be kind enough to tell me to whom these belong?'

'My husband, Akbar.'

'Was he wearing them on the night Rajiv was shot?'

'I don't remember. Why does it matter?' I ask belligerently.

'I see. However, if he were, then his fingerprints wouldn't have been on the gun, would they?'

I was right in my assessment. I understand the game, and the dice might roll in my favour. After all, I'm within the snake's reach, and the bite now signifies the end of the game for me. I must remain alert and vigilant. Guarded, as they say.

'Mrs Khan, I assume you must have known that your husband Akbar's fingerprints would invariably be on the gun; it was his gun, and he was the only one who had ever handled it before Friday evening, wasn't he?'

I stare at her. I don't reply.

'Would you like to reconsider, Mrs Khan? Take as long as you need to ensure you recall every detail accurately.'

'What are you proposing, ACP Jha?' Sid inquires.

'I am not suggesting or proposing anything, Mr Dhariwal, and I believe it is time I asked you and Mrs Dhariwal to leave. Please.'

'What if we decline to?'

I want to rise and give Sid a warm hug for continuing to support me.

'Please do not compel me to use force to remove you and Mrs Dhariwal. I can request my constables to escort you out if you do not leave of your own accord.'

'You're crossing the line, ACP Jha. You've pretended all along that Anush was here as either a victim or merely a witness when, in fact, you were treating her as a suspect. Therefore, I believe we should halt this interrogation immediately until—'

'Until?'

'Anush,' Sid is speaking to me now, 'don't answer anything she asks. Whatever you say could be used against you. I wouldn't trust ACP Jha for a second longer. I'm calling the lawyer I mentioned. Do not say a word until the lawyer arrives.'

I look at ACP Jha.

'That's entirely your prerogative, Mrs Khan,' she says, but I know she doesn't mean a word of it.

From the corner of my eye, I can see that Sid has walked away and is making a call to someone. His expression and the animated conversation suggest that he is emphasising the urgency to the person on the other end of the line.

'Don't say a word, Anush,' he says upon his return. 'ACP Jha, I've been advised by Anushka's lawyer that we should leave straight away. Unless you have a warrant for Anushka, you cannot stop us; that's her *right*.'

I don't want any more *tamasha* in Sid and Aanya's presence. They've seen enough. They've heard enough. I need to play my game all by myself now. 'Aanya,' I say, 'I kindly ask you and Sid to leave, please. There has been some misunderstanding, and it's best if I have a chat with ACP Jha alone—'

'Are you sure? Don't feel any pressure, Anush.' Sid's politeness and deference have vanished. His tone is hostile, his eyes filled with fury. 'ACP sahiba, you know as well as I do that you're playing with fire here, and therefore, we are taking Anushka with us.'

'Obstructing a public servant in the discharge of public functions is a criminal offence, Mr Dhariwal. Under Section 186 of the penal statute, the charge carries a potential imprisonment of up to three months. You have been warned, in case you weren't aware. So I ask that you refrain from interfering with these proceedings. Should the need arise, we shall be taking Mrs Khan to the Saket Police Station with us. Please ensure her lawyer presents themselves at the police station with the relevant documentation. According to Mrs Khan's wishes, she is not obliged to answer any of our questions until her lawyer arrives. Do you have any further questions?' She remains equally discourteous and succinct. The pretence of friendliness has entirely evaporated from the room now.

Suddenly, I am reminded of an idiom my mother used to say quite often: '*Anush, hammam mein to sabhi nange hote hain.*' (Everyone gets naked in the bath.)

I gaze at her in disbelief. Anxious. Afraid. She has rolled the dice; she's revealed her cards. I haven't, but I shall not do that in the presence of my friends.

Sid doesn't argue with the ACP any more. They've gone out on a limb, but they are not going to face imprisonment for me. 'We're not leaving you, Anush; we'll wait in the car,' he says as they walk out.

'I thought so,' the ACP murmurs.

You can't always get what you want, as Mick Jagger said. Things don't always go to plan. All I ever wished for was to be free. But it was a stillborn dream, as I now realise, because here I am, waiting for my lawyer to arrive, sitting with ACP Jha in my own living room, and yet it feels like a prison. The thought of spending the night in the lock-up is daunting. My prospects after this night don't seem very bright either.

Forty

'What do you have to say?' ACP Jha asks after Aanya and Sid leave.

'About what? I'm not sure what you're asking.'

'About the gloves.'

'I still don't understand what you want me to say. You found Akbar's gloves in our bedroom – how does that change anything?'

Fortunately, the lawyer – the one Sid called before leaving – arriving at this opportune moment feels like a lifeline. Samir Bhargava is a lawyer straight out of a storybook. He wears an expensive black coat in a silk-linen blend, along with a white shirt and white trousers, complemented by a silk tie. He is tall – around five foot nine – with curly salt-and-pepper hair and camel-coloured eyes, and a permanent smile painted on his face. According to the law, he is permitted to spend some time alone with me, to hear my side of the story before ACP Jha questions me in his presence. He asks ACP Jha to leave the room, and she obliges, stating she will meet us at the Saket Police Station.

Bhargava first insists that I keep him as his advocate on record. He then provides paperwork for me to sign, which I do without inquiring about the cost of his services. I am confident that Sid has already handled those negotiations.

After the formalities, he takes out a writing pad. 'Mrs Khan, I've read about this case in the papers, but I don't think you should have any significant cause for concern here.' His voice is that of a smoker: raspy yet authoritative. 'We have limited time before we head to Saket to see ACP Jha, but remember, I'll be with you. Whenever she asks you a question that you're uncomfortable answering, you can always reply with "No comments". As for me, if I find any of her questions particularly incriminating, or if she tries to lead you, I'll give you a nudge, and you can say that you wish to consult me before responding. It's well within your rights to decline to answer and request more time—'

'And what are my options?'

'My team back at the office is already preparing the paperwork to apply for anticipatory bail in case ACP Jha has any evidence that she might spring on us.'

'How long would that take?'

'Probably a few hours.'

'So she could arrest me when we go to the police station?'

'No. I mean, she can only make an arrest if she possesses any tangible evidence that incriminates you, and even if that's the case, we will get you out within hours.'

My heart sinks. I have heard dreadful stories about lock-ups and prisons. Are the cells six by eight or eight by ten? 'But I am innocent.'

Samir nods. I cannot determine whether he is convinced of my innocence or not.

'Do you not believe me?'

'I do, but Anushka – may I call you Anushka?' I nod, and he goes on. 'You must understand that you or anyone in your position would claim to be innocent, even if they were not. Ultimately, it matters little what I believe or do not believe; we need to consider the evidence that ACP Jha possesses.'

We talk for another twenty minutes to solidify our plan before deciding to leave for the police station. Sid and Aanya are still sitting in their car, waiting. They must have seen ACP Jha leave, but they didn't come in since Bhim Singh was still at the door. I think she didn't leave the constable behind to stop my friends from entering my house; she left him here so that I wouldn't bolt. However, it may be that I am just paranoid. When we arrive at Saket Police Station, Advocate Bhargava and I are shown into a small room and asked to wait for ACP Jha. The room is no larger than the pantry next to my kitchen at Sainik Farms. A table stands in the middle, with two chairs on each side. Contrary to what the films depict, there is no unidirectional glass window. The chairs are grimy, and their cushions are paper-thin. Naturally, this is not Le Méridien. Advocate Bhargava and I have already covered everything there was to discuss, so we simply sit and stare at the wall before us.

Ten minutes pass before there is a knock at the door, and before we can respond, it swings open, revealing ACP Kamala Jha accompanied by a junior officer. He is unfamiliar, someone I have not seen or met before.

'This is Inspector Gupta,' she says with a nonchalant air, as if she were introducing me to someone at a cocktail party. Inspector Gupta carries a bag slung over his shoulder.

'ACP Jha, do you possess an arrest warrant for my client?' Bhargava rises from his chair and strides towards my side of the table. It strikes me that it's us against them now.

'Not yet.'

'So she is free to leave any time she wishes to.'

'Of course she can.'

'Is she a suspect?' Bhargava asks.

'Yes.'

'And what crime is she accused of?'

She gestures towards Inspector Gupta, who is carrying a file. He opens the file, extracts the first sheet, and hands it to Bhargava. I can see the colour rising in his face as he reads it.

'How is that possible?' he exclaims. I shift closer to him and glance at the paper in his hand. She's charged me with the homicide of Rajiv Pant and...But before I can read any further, she snatches the paper from Bhargava's hand. What a bitch!

'We have much ground to cover, Advocate Bhargava. Shall we begin?' she asks, taking a seat. Gupta settles next to her. 'Inspector Gupta...' she adds, and Gupta retrieves a small tape recorder from his bag and places it on the desk between us.

'First interview of Mrs Anushka Khan as a suspect in the murder of Mr Rajiv Pant. In the room with her are Advocate Samir Bhargava, ACP Kamala Jha and Inspector Raj Gupta.' Gupta introduces us to the tape and provides some additional cautions before ACP Jha begins.

'Mrs Khan, I believed your story for a long time because I was lacking a minor detail. These gloves. How could they have gunshot residue if they weren't used to fire a gun?'

'Akbar could have left them at the scene before he fled?' Bhargava's response sounds more like an apology than an explanation.

'It cannot be. For one, if Akbar left the gloves at the scene of the crime before he fled, how did they end up in Mrs Khan's locked bedroom? She was comatose by the time someone broke down the bedroom door, so no one could have done that. Besides, there was no one else at home. Secondly, Akbar wasn't there that evening because he had died the day before. Isn't that right, Mrs Khan?'

She gazes at me, and I gaze back at her.

'Mrs Khan, I've heard your version of the story, which you concocted—'

'Objection.'

'Mr Bhargava, save your objections for the courtroom. This is a police station, and none of your cunning lawyer tactics will yield the result you desire.' The ACP is as stern as she can be without raising her voice. 'I kindly ask you not to interrupt while I am speaking to Mrs Khan. We are on tape, so if I step out of line, it will be recorded, and you may address it in court. I trust I have made myself clear.'

There is silence in the room for a minute.

'So, Mrs Khan, let's review the statements you've provided to the police so far.' She takes the file from Inspector Gupta and examines it. 'You mentioned that someone smashed your head against the mirror, causing you to fall, after which you ran into your bedroom and locked the door from the inside. You then heard a gunshot before someone began banging aggressively on the bedroom door while you called the police. You also stated that no one entered the bedroom until help arrived, broke the door open and carried you to the ambulance. Am I correct?'

I nod.

'We need a verbal response for the tape, Mrs Khan,' she says, gesturing towards the recorder.

'Yes.'

'Inspector Gupta,' she says.

Inspector Gupta opens his bag and extracts the same set of gloves from the evidence bag that was presented to me at my home.

'Exhibit RMC/12, presented to the suspect and her lawyer, consists of a pair of tan and brown leather gloves discovered in a chest of drawers, concealed beneath women's lingerie in Mrs Khan's bedroom. For the record, do you recognise these gloves, Mrs Khan?'

I glance at Bhargava, but there's little I can do now. I've already admitted I do. 'Yes.'

'And to whom do these gloves belong, Mrs Khan?'

'My husband, Akbar.'

'Could you explain how they ended up buried beneath your lingerie in your bedroom?'

'ACP Jha, my client and her husband lived under the same roof. They did not keep secrets, nor did they lock their wardrobes, so Akbar Khan could have stored his gloves in my client's drawers at any time—'

'Except...Akbar Khan did not keep them there at any time. The gloves were stored in Mrs Khan's chest of drawers in her bedroom *after* the gun was fired. There is gunshot residue on them to support this, Mr Bhargava. And since no one entered the bedroom after Mrs Khan locked it from the inside, how did these gloves end up in there unless she allowed someone into the bedroom after Rajiv Pant was shot? The only plausible alternative is that she brought the gloves into the bedroom herself and left them there. Which is it, Mrs Khan?'

'I don't know.'

'Please, Mrs Khan, stop the charade now.'

I remain silent. I had informed Advocate Bhargava of everything I needed to express without letting it slip that I had studied law. I did not want him to view me as someone who had contemplated the situation for the past fortnight and crafted a response in anticipation of the police discovering the gloves and this scenario arising. I presented it as an impromptu outburst and, to the best of my knowledge, he found my explanation quite plausible, which sufficed for me.

'Let me explain the sequence of events as I see them. I've been thinking of the haadsaa at your place since the day I met you. My theory is that there was no one in the house that day except you and Rajiv. Both of you were drinking – Rajiv's autopsy report is in the file for you to see later, Mr Bhargava. Maybe you hadn't planned it, but some altercation occurred between the two of you, and you knew where Akbar kept his gun. But you were smart. You found his gloves, put them on and shot Rajiv. Then you panicked. You banged your head against the mirror to make it look like you were beaten. You then ran to your bedroom, hid the gloves, consumed sleeping pills with more alcohol and waited fifteen minutes for the drugs to take effect before calling the police. And while you called the emergency hotline, you banged the door to make it sound like you were under threat. How's that for a theory?'

I feel numb. Why is ACP Jha so intent on accusing me of something for which she has no evidence?

'It's good, ACP Jha,' Advocate Bhargava eventually asserts, 'but the issue remains that this is merely that: a theory. A highly imaginative, convoluted theory. I know you mentioned that this is a police station and not a courtroom, but please tell me you do not intend to take this to court, for I can assure you that no judge would ever allow such wild speculation in a court of law. You do not possess a shred of evidence that my client did any of that. How can you genuinely believe that story? My client, Mrs Anushka Khan, has been a victim of domestic abuse. Yes, she made the mistake of stepping outside the boundaries of marriage, and she has paid for it. However, that is not a crime in itself. You do not have any tangible evidence against my client—'

'Really? Can you explain how Akbar's gloves, which had gunshot residue on them, ended up in a locked bedroom and found their way into Mrs Khan's lingerie drawer?' As ACP Jha answers Advocate Bhargava, she looks me directly in the eye, challenging me.

Bhargava lets out a guffaw.

'Is there a problem, Mr Bhargava?' ACP Jha is evidently unimpressed by Bhargava's disdainful snicker at her carefully crafted narrative.

'Not *a* problem, ACP Jha; I don't have just one but numerous issues with your theory. Your theory has more holes than a vintage hand-me-down sieve.' Bhargava briefly glances at me, smiles and then turns to ACP Jha. 'Your theory is nothing more than a collection of suspicions and conjectures that I could unravel in my sleep.

'To begin with, my client, Mrs Khan, was taken to hospital immediately following the haadsaa on the 7th of July, and the premises were declared a crime scene by the police, cordoned off and sealed. From the 7th until yesterday evening, which was the 20th, the house has been under your control – visited, searched and investigated solely by you and your teams. Am I right in saying that your expert investigators did not uncover these gloves during the first twelve days—'

'That's because we didn't have enough information. Our prime suspect, until we discovered his body, was Akbar. Things changed once we found his corpse.'

'How does the discovery of Akbar's body change anything?'

I knew Bhargava was aware of the answer. He was merely pretending to be obtuse. Now, he was the one posing questions, building the narrative I had imagined he would.

'Because we began searching for Akbar's killer,' the ACP asserted firmly.

'But that is not what you are accusing my client of, is it? You are accusing my client of murdering Mr Rajiv Pant.'

That is why I wished to become a lawyer. The arguments presented by lawyers sound like pure poetry to my ears. They suspend reality, make listeners doubt themselves and push the debate to the brink, prompting those who are convinced of their beliefs to question themselves. I could hug Advocate Bhargava at this moment. Of all those who have fought my corner thus far, he is poised to be the biggest game-changer. Man of the match!

'And,' Bhargava continues, 'these gloves you discovered in my client's locked bedroom drawer...please remember that the bedroom was locked from the inside on 7th July and after it was opened, has remained in police custody until the 20th—'

'That doesn't change anything. No one except the police had access to the house.'

'But don't you see ACP Jha that that little fact changes everything? Your team discovered these gloves more than twelve days after my client left the house and did not return. Someone could have easily slipped in and placed these gloves in her drawer to implicate her, as she did not put them there.'

'Mr Bhargava,' ACP Jha says, furious, 'are you suggesting that someone from the police force has planted these to incriminate Mrs Khan?' She is now seething with rage. If she could, she would throttle Bhargava right here.

'I did not accuse anyone, ACP Jha. I am simply posing questions that any lawyer ought to ask. What you have is not even circumstantial evidence; perhaps it is merely a hunch, but that is hardly substantial in light of the contrary—'

'Save this argument for the courtroom, Mr Bhargava. If you suggest that a member of my team deliberately placed these gloves in her bedroom to frame Mrs Khan, I assure you that I will sue for slander. We are the police, not some scum you are used to representing in court.'

'Not to mention...' Bhargava ignores ACP Jha's tone and carries on regardless, '...your team packed up their tents and vacated the property last evening, leaving the house unsecured overnight. Who knows who could have entered the premises?'

'This meeting is over.' ACP Jha is having none of it. 'And you, Mrs Khan, I suggest you start speaking soon. The meeting has been terminated,' she reiterates to Inspector Gupta, who turns off the tape recorder.

As Gupta packs everything and leaves the room, Kamala glares at me, unblinking. 'Mrs Khan is free to leave for now, but I shall get her. I know she killed both of them,' she says.

'And yet you have no evidence, ACP Jha. My client is a housewife, a victim of domestic abuse, and not a member of some mafia who orchestrated a double homicide so meticulously that she left not a single shred of evidence behind.'

'What if we find her DNA in the gloves?'

'So, a wife wore her husband's gloves. Could it be that the husband asked her to try them on? My client wouldn't be the first to wear her husband's gloves, nor would she be the last. It proves nothing.'

ACP Jha gets up to leave.

'By the way, ACP Jha,' Advocate Bhargava rises as well. 'My client has faced harassment from the police even while she was in hospital, recovering from her ordeal and injuries. The police visited her in plain clothes at unusual hours while she was unwell, a situation that has been captured on camera. This prompts me to question whether the police intended to railroad her even before the investigation had commenced. And then the gloves appear at a most convenient time – who can say who placed them there? I believe my client wishes to file a complaint with the Police Complaints Authority regarding this misconduct.'

ACP Jha is aware of which police officer came to see me in the hospital, the individual against whom the complaint would be lodged, and the consequences for her career. For a change, Kamala Jha is at ninety-five, and the snake is at ninety-eight.

FRIDAY, 5TH JULY

Forty-One

Sometimes, even the best intentions do not produce the desired results. Advocate Bhargava contacted me first thing in the morning to inform me that ACP Kamala Jha had submitted a new application to the magistrate to revoke my anticipatory bail, citing the discovery of new evidence, specifically the gloves, which had not been disclosed prior to the anticipatory bail being granted.

'Is it merely the gloves?' I inquire.

'Is there anything else I should know about?' I can feel the tension in Bhargava's voice.

'I don't know what I don't know, Samir. Given how this ACP has conducted this investigation, I wouldn't be surprised if she presents more superficial evidence to frame me.'

'Why is she so unwaveringly focused on you?'

'I haven't a clue. You'll need to ask her about that.'

'Anyway, I'll collect you at ten-thirty from Aanya's house.'

'OK.'

As our Sainik Farm residence has once again been cordoned off, I had little choice but to return with Sid and Aanya for the night. We had discussed Kamala's latest trick of pulling Akbar's gloves from my drawer. Who knew who had placed them there. And when.

***

Despite her irksome determination to pursue me, I cannot help but respect ACP Kamala Jha. I hadn't anticipated her submitting this new application to revoke my bail, especially after Bhargava hinted to her that I was prepared to lodge a complaint against her – a complaint that could jeopardise her career. However, that did not deter her; she remained steadfast in her resolve. She dared to roll the dice at ninety-five. She did not fret. She did not fear the consequences. Or perhaps she was convinced I was guilty.

I understand her motivation, however. Being a woman in a role created solely for men must be quite challenging. During my law studies, I completed a module on policing, procedures and governance. To my horror, I discovered that some of the older police stations – those that had yet to be renovated and where there was neither the budget nor the inclination to update them – lacked any toilet facilities for women. It screamed, 'Women are not welcome,' *far* more than the authorities were willing to acknowledge.

Integrating into an organisation as patriarchal as the police force was no easy task. Moreover, we learned it wasn't only in India. The police worldwide remain male-dominated, even in developed countries such as the US and the UK.

But so is society at large: simply misogynistic. Akbar abused me because he held all the power. So did Rajiv. Some may disagree with how it unfolded, but both of them received what they deserved.

Solving this double homicide case and securing a conviction within weeks would be a significant achievement for Kamala. However, as much as I would like to assist another woman, the cost of this would be my life.

As Aanya had advised, I wore a white sari. A grieving wife.

The magistrate, Mr Chirag Singh, seemed disinterested in being present. Perhaps he had to cancel a round of golf to attend; I can't be certain. A short man seated in a tall chair wore glasses resembling tiny CDs. His expression showed no emotion. Once the case number was announced and everyone was introduced, he raised his hand to indicate that he had already reviewed the file submitted by the police. In his opinion, the gloves were rightly identified as a new discovery, warranting a reconsideration of the bail previously granted.

My heart sank. Was the snake finally about to bite me?

The ACP and my advocate presented their arguments for the next twenty minutes. However, the police's failure to secure my property overnight disrupted the case. Bhargava emphasised that it would be a travesty of justice if the police detained me, a grieving widow, without providing tangible, uncontaminated evidence.

As a result, Chirag Singh ji ruled in my favour. He concurred that the gloves could not be accepted as they would be deemed tainted.

Yes, Kamala was entitled to file a case, and the verdict would need to be determined by a judge.

But for now, I was free.

I was also relieved that Samir didn't have to tarnish Kamala's image with dirty paint. We had both evaded the snake, although there would still be a trial, and the police would carry on with their investigation.

Forty-Two

I'm not sure whether I should apologise, as I haven't been entirely honest with you.

What I've shared with you thus far has been rather one-dimensional. Specifically, it reflects how I wanted to present my perspective: how I felt and what it should have been. I may have intentionally overlooked a minor detail or two. I might have even got away with it if there hadn't been someone as deeply involved in Rajiv Pant's homicide as ACP Kamala Jha. She doesn't know the entire story, but given her tenacity, the snake fangs glare at me from ninety-eight.

I wasn't dishonest when I told the police that Akbar and I were home alone, after the servants had left for the day, drinking. I simply provided the incorrect time and day. A straightforward chronological chicanery, I admit. We didn't start drinking around four in the afternoon, as I stated; we actually began at around seven-thirty. Furthermore, it wasn't Saturday evening; it was Friday evening. Akbar returned home at seven, well after all the servants had departed for the weekend. Therefore, no one could ever know if the first drink was poured at seven-thirty on Friday or at four on Saturday afternoon. There was no one to see – *or not see* – Akbar's car at the house either.

I prepared the drinks, not Akbar. A glass of tonic water for me, with a splash of gin. A double measure of Jack Daniel's with cola for Akbar, just as he preferred. Another subtle misstatement, but it matters when you consider the subtext here. If I were the one making the drinks, how could Akbar have drugged me? When you start to think along those lines, I'm sure you can make the imaginative leap and conclude that if anyone had the opportunity to lace the drinks with sleeping pills, it was me, not Akbar. Yes, that was our plan: mine and Rajiv's.

I didn't mix anything into the first drink; it seemed too risky in case he noticed the taste was slightly off. After the first large drink, I urged him to finish those that followed quickly as I had already downed my tonic water. I discreetly slipped the first super-strength sleeping tablet that Rajiv had given me into Akbar's second drink, followed by two more in his third. That was all that was needed to knock him out.

Akbar complained of a headache and wanted to lie down. I didn't want to overdose him; the plan was to help him sleep. The tablets had begun to take effect by half-past nine, and by ten that evening, he was sound asleep, snoring.

'Has the staff left?' As arranged, I was in the bathroom at five minutes past six in the evening when Rajiv had called.

'I think so. I heard the door shut while I was inside. Let me go down and check. Are you sure?'

'Of course, I am certain, Anush. You know I would do anything for you. I loathe the fact that you have to sleep with that monster when it is me you're in love with. We've discussed this before. He's a brute; he doesn't understand how precious you are, and the way he abuses you physically and mentally is abhorrent. We have been devising and fine-tuning the entire plan in detail for the past few weeks. We should do this. Are you still in two minds, Anush?'

'No.'

'Good. Then let's carry on with our plan. I'll be there by eleven.'

Of course, the neighbours hadn't seen Rajiv since Friday afternoon, as he had been at the farm, clearing the garage, checking the freezer, changing the locks. A month ago, Rajiv had rented some farmland – an acre of barren land with a fence and a garage. A week ago, we had decided to buy a freezer with the money I had given him – Akbar's money. I had handed the cash to Rajiv, but he had clearly pocketed it and purchased the machine on his credit card. What on earth was that idiot thinking? After planning it so meticulously to keep the freezer's location under wraps – we had even decided that Rajiv would provide our home address and request delivery on a specific day when we knew Akbar would be at the office. Rajiv had also hired a van with an extra pair of hands. The freezer was delivered out of sight within the gate, away from the property, so that the servants wouldn't see it being swiftly carted away. The freezer was then transported to the garage at the farmland. The entire ruse had been orchestrated in case someone caught wind of the purchase and questioned the shopkeeper. Buying it on a credit card almost guaranteed that the police would uncover his transaction.

Rajiv knew the passcode for our front gate, so he drove in with his headlights switched off. As I could see him from the window, he didn't need to ring the doorbell.

***

Akbar lay unconscious when Rajiv placed a pillow over his face and smothered him. Ghastly, I must admit, but we both wanted Akbar out of the way. We aimed to dispose of Akbar so that we could be together. Akbar's widow would inherit all the money, and in time, I would, apparently, fall in love with Akbar's school friend who consoled me in my hour of distress.

Corny, but it would work.

Akbar wasn't as light as I had expected. I should have known by the way he could carry me, push me around and rough me up, but his corpse seemed even heavier. However, the two of us carried him down and loaded him into the boot of his Mercedes. Rajiv drove Akbar's car to the farmland that nobody besides me knew he had rented, and I followed him in his car. Our plan was to tell everyone that Akbar had gone to this ancestral property for a few weeks. It had happened before so no one would suspect anything untoward immediately. When he didn't return after a month, I would lodge a missing person's complaint. With a month gone, it would be difficult, if not impossible, for the police to trace back Akbar's last steps, or mine, to come after me.

The ACP discovered that CCTV footage captured both Akbar's and Rajiv's cars. However, this did not constitute evidence of foul play. The two were friends, and it was possible they went somewhere together. Why should that raise any concerns?

It didn't take us long to unload Akbar's body and put it in the freezer, where we assumed it would be safe for a few months. We decided we'd figure out later how to dispose of it. It wasn't something we needed to do right away.

The ACP was correct that there were two passengers in Rajiv's car on the return.

Fortunately, it was dark, and the cameras were positioned so high that they generated grainy images that were unrecognisable. Otherwise, I would have been discovered a few days earlier.

The idea always was that I'd say Akbar left on Saturday afternoon, not on Friday, so if his car was captured on camera on Friday, it wouldn't matter.

When we returned home after securing Akbar's body and his car in the garage, the atmosphere was tense. We didn't speak; we merely went to sleep in separate bedrooms. I didn't want Rajiv's DNA within me, on me or anywhere near me.

Forty-Three

Infidelity. It is predominantly cowardice that drives individuals into illicit affairs. Unable to rectify what was amiss in my relationship, I sought solace elsewhere. With Rajiv, I was so blinded by passion that I overlooked his true character.

I had no idea that Akbar was operating a hawala shop. I was truly shocked to discover that Rajiv was my husband's partner in an unlawful business.

I also didn't know that Rajiv would turn out to be a pervert. I didn't know about his discreet photographs of me taken during our most intimate moments, I swear. He exposed his true self the afternoon after Akbar's murder. He didn't take them out of any appreciation for my body or my sexual prowess. He had taken photographs of me as leverage in the event I turned against him. If I did that, he told me, he would use them to blackmail me. It was a double whammy when he told me about his backup plan. It shouldn't have come as a shock to me that he didn't love me.

'I can still use the photographs, Anush,' he joked, but I could sense that he was asserting his place and authority in this new relationship.

'How do you mean?' I thought I had found an escape from my abusive husband, only to realise I was being blackmailed by the man I had naïvely assumed was in love with me.

'I can make you do anything now. Don't forget, it doesn't matter if Akbar isn't around; I can still leak these photographs to the media. They'll pay good money for a body like yours.'

'You won't do that, I know.' I closed my eyes to imagine what would happen if he did. One of my first thoughts was to run away and hide. The obvious question was, where would I go? I couldn't just up and leave and return to Jamnagar. My parents were long gone; I had no home and no money. If I went to Jamnagar without any funds, what would I do? Clean utensils in other people's houses, wash and iron their clothes, or use my body like my mother?

'Don't be so certain, you little slut.' It was now afternoon, and he had already helped himself to a drink from the bar. 'Once everything is sorted in a month or two, you will get access to all of Akbar's assets but I will be the one in control. I will manage the money and I will manage you. Of course, you and I will be together, but I must control everything, not you. And do not ever try to be clever with me. If I send the photographs to the police, I'm sure they'll surmise that you had a strong motive to have your husband killed and make his body disappear. And if that isn't sufficient, I can provide them with the body as well.'

I realised then that I had made a dreadful mistake in trusting this wicked scoundrel. He had betrayed me. I had believed him, and he deceived me into thinking he loved me. It didn't matter who actually owned the entire property as long as we were together. In any case, we had to stand by one another to execute our plan. One of the tasks was to use Akbar's phone to call Rajiv so that, if and when the police began their investigation, they would believe Akbar was still alive on Saturday evening. This turned out to be useful later for another reason, but that was merely luck.

'I need to take a leak. Take off that fancy pink dress and be on your knees when I return. You give good head,' he said, winking before heading to the loo.

I don't know how much Rajiv trusted me then, because I didn't trust myself.

When he was in the loo, I slipped into Akbar's study. The rest unfolded precisely as ACP Kamala Jha had surmised.

I knew where Akbar kept his gun. I knew it would be covered with Akbar's fingerprints. I took off all my clothes, put on Akbar's gloves and as I came out in my underwear, Rajiv was in the entrance foyer. Maybe he came after me to check, but before he could say anything, I shot him. With no clothes on, there was no gunshot residue on me. He died almost instantly. Kamala was correct in her assessment: it was then that I panicked. I had a quick gin and tonic to calm my nerves and came up with the plausible story of an altercation between my husband and my lover. The call was already made from Akbar's phone to Rajiv's. I knew it would work to my advantage. I put my dress back on, and it took me two strong drinks to gather enough courage to smash my own head against the mirror. I felt warm blood on my forehead; I knew I had hurt myself deep enough. I consumed the rest of the sleeping pills with lots of gin – I had given Akbar three, and I still had seven left in the strip – then ran into my bedroom and made that call. I knew if I got help within an hour, they'd flush out my stomach and I'd survive. The only mistake I made was not throwing the gloves on Rajiv's body when I discarded both mobile phones and the gun.

Forty-Four

A little embellishment.

An additional fact.

A tiny omission.

And suddenly, the truth is no longer the truth.

What is so morally superior about 'truth', anyway? It's merely a perspective, isn't it? You might view certain individuals as evil, believing that what they did was wrong, and perhaps they made compromises along the way or lost the plot completely. You are entitled to your opinion, as *your* perspective is your prerogative. All I can suggest in their defence is that you should reserve your judgement until you've heard the story in its entirety.

Sometimes, a minor detail can sway the most unyielding convictions.

***

You may wonder about some gaps in my story. There are none. I had already taken some semi-clad photographs of myself two weeks ago and texted them to Sid using Akbar's phone, then deleted the messages. However, it was for an entirely different purpose. I knew Akbar suspected I was having an affair with Rajiv. If something were to happen to me, or if I filed for divorce, I wanted someone else to corroborate how vile Akbar was, that he had abused and hurt me because he knew about my affair. It served as a kind of insurance, but when Rajiv died, I realised it would be useful in providing the police with a reason for the fight between the two men.

I had intended to play dumb. If you go back and check my account, you will see that I've never intentionally lied. At best, I am guilty of a little embellishment, an additional fact or a minor omission. It was my perspective. What is so morally superior about 'truth', anyway? It's merely a point of view, isn't it?

Yes, I manipulated certain individuals, but they were willing participants. I presented a hypothesis, offered another perspective, a different angle, and encouraged others to consider those theories until they appeared convinced of their complete validity. Even better, there were occasions when they took it upon themselves to argue for them as though they were their own ideas. I simply sowed the seeds and allowed them to flourish.

I flirted with Dr Aryan Yadav and shared my account of deprivation. He was willing to chaperone me, even posing his own questions to the police and objecting to some of their awkward inquiries when ACP Kamala first came to see me at the hospital. I then shifted my focus to Sid, as I quickly realised he would be a better advocate to represent my interests when Kamala came to question me again.

Incidentally, Monica was the first person to visit me in the hospital. I tried to slip into our conversation that the only way Akbar might have evaded capture was if he had outside assistance, that there could have been a third person at our doorstep the other day, but she didn't take the bait. I didn't reiterate my theory to her. I didn't want to come across as overly enthusiastic. I let it drop, then.

I attempted to introduce a theory that Akbar might have gone to Jaipur. This theory briefly gained momentum as they deemed it worthwhile to check Chandigarh airport as well, but it soon fizzled out. By then, I had become aware of Akbar's hawala shop.

The fact that he was involved in hawala and that Rajiv was his trusted pigeon was news to me before, but it opened a new door and corroborated my story. It gave me the additional weight required to impress upon Sid and Aanya that the likelihood of a third person being present outside our residence on Saturday evening – perhaps to seek revenge or due to a deal gone wrong – was nearly certain. Sid took the baton and ran with it. He was not only quick to accept it, but he also advanced it, enhanced it and even named the third person: Mr X.

He convinced ACP Jha of the existence of a third man on the evening of the murder. Mr X was, of course, a fabrication. However, once Mr X entered Sid's narrative, the theory took on a life of its own. Mr X became an almost foregone conclusion for a time, and that suited me just fine. Mr X *might* have bashed my head; he intended to kill me after shooting Rajiv, and he even came knocking at my door. Akbar had fled to save his life because he knew Mr X would come after him, or perhaps Akbar pursued Mr X. Or maybe they escaped together? I was pleased to see that the ACP was landing on the wrong runway – I had pointed it out to her – until she discovered the gloves, making my involvement glaringly obvious to her.

I made a blunder, nearly losing my temper when Vasu suggested that Rajiv might have bought the freezer to conceal a corpse. I didn't want anyone to suspect that, so I had to quell that thought immediately, but my aggressive reaction could have drawn attention. For that reason, I swiftly apologised, changed direction and broke down.

You might think I shed false tears all the time, but let me tell you that despite all I have done, I was traumatised and shaken. I had lost my husband – though he was abusive – no matter how he died, and my lover, who was only interested in my husband's money.

The on-demand tears were a consequence of that. If you lost both the men you once loved within twenty-four hours, you experience a sense of loss so profound that it brings you to tears every time you reflect on the situation you've created for yourself: an adulteress, a murderer, a black widow.

You might wonder who planted the GPS tracker in my car. The police didn't do it, and they would never find any app or software on any device that tracked my car's movements. The data wasn't being sent to any device. I know this because I purchased it myself. With cash. And installed it. It wasn't sending signals anywhere. It was merely placed there to demonstrate that Akbar was wicked enough to keep tabs on me. What more reason does a wife need to file for divorce besides an abusive husband who checks on his wife using devices and also circulates sleazy pictures of her to his friends? In retrospect, I should have asked for a divorce rather than going along with Rajiv's idea. I think that with a bit of luck, I might have escaped the murder charge, too, but then, if luck had been on my side, Rajiv might not have double-crossed me. If luck had favoured me, this homicide case would never have been handed over to the Saket Police Station; someone intelligent and tenacious like ACP Kamala Jha wouldn't have investigated it, but there you go…

For now the snake remains at ninety-eight, but I am convinced I'll beat it because the alternative is too horrible to imagine.

I am not proud of what I did, nor do I believe my actions were right. However, every person – especially a woman – faces this dilemma at least once in their lifetime, when they have little choice but to resort to extreme measures to eliminate a threat when no other options remain. Believe me, this is not a stunt promoting post-purchase rationalisation or a masterclass on self-justification. I will pay for my sins one day, but I won't allow Kamala or anyone else in this world to decide my fate.

Acknowledgements

This story is far from what I had originally written. After writing the first draft, I changed the beginning, the end and everything in between. And, as though that wasn't enough, I changed the title too. Haadsaa means an incident, and like everything else in life, incidents can be happy or sad.

This book wouldn't have been complete without Nidhi, who always encourages me to kill a few more characters and add some extra twists to make the story more engaging. She has truly become my partner in crime.

Thank you to my friend Malcolm Lauder, who edited the final draft. I am blessed to have a friend who always has my back when it comes to proofreading.

I am always grateful to Mita Kapur and Siyahi for helping me shape the story. Additionally, this book wouldn't be in your hands without the support of the editorial team at Bloomsbury. I sincerely thank all the wonderful people mentioned above for contributing to my growth as a writer.

And, of course, there would be little sense in writing a story if it were not for you, my lovely readers. I hope you enjoy reading *Haadsaa* as much as I enjoyed writing it.

Acknowledgement

[illegible]

About the Author

Vish Dhamija is an international award-winning British Indian crime fiction writer with twelve novels to his name. He is the first writer of Indian origin to win the prestigious Prix Cognac 2024 du Meilleur Roman International (Cognac Prize 2024 for Best International – Crime) at the Festival Polar de Cognac for his novel *Le Magnat*, published in India as *The Mogul*. The French press has also celebrated him as one of the five crime writers not to be missed.

Often referred to as 'India's John Grisham', Dhamija stands out as the only writer of Indian origin to be listed among the major legal thriller authors in the world. His books are highly sought after for adaptation. *Bhendi Bazaar* will soon be brought to screen and four of Dhamija's other works are currently in various stages of screen adaptation.

Vish Dhamija can be reached on Instagram at @vish_dhamija, on Facebook at www.facebook.com/vishdhamija and via email at vishdhamija@gmail.com.